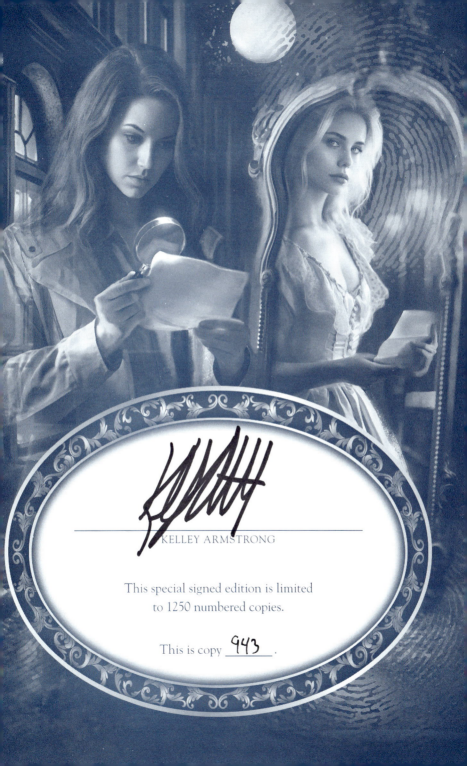

KELLEY ARMSTRONG

This special signed edition is limited to 1250 numbered copies.

This is copy 943.

SCHEMES & SCANDALS

SCHEMES & SCANDALS
A RIP THROUGH TIME NOVELLA

KELLEY ARMSTRONG

Subterranean Press 2024

Schemes & Scandals
Copyright © 2024 by KLA Fricke Inc.
All rights reserved.

Dust jacket illustration
Copyright © 2024 by Maurizio Manzieri.
All rights reserved.

Interior design
Copyright © 2024 by Desert Isle Design, LLC.
All rights reserved.

First Edition

ISBN
978-1-64524-207-9

Subterranean Press
PO Box 190106
Burton, MI 48519

subterraneanpress.com

Manufactured in the United States of America

Author's Note

Charles Dickens's farewell tour *did* take him to Edinburgh in 1869. He *did* need to reschedule the first date (February 19) due to a broken foot. However, the rescheduled date was only a week later. I've trusted readers will allow me the creative license of moving the rescheduled appearance to accommodate Mallory's timeline.

ON THE first of December, I walk into the townhouse library and announce, "I believe it's time to discuss Christmas."

I've been very patient about the whole thing, considering it's my first Victorian Christmas. I spent the last one in Vancouver…in 2018. That spring, I ended up in 1869 Edinburgh, which is a very long story, the short version being that I crossed into the body of a nineteen-year-old housemaid working for Dr. Duncan Gray and his widowed chemist sister, Isla. Gray is an undertaker with degrees in both surgery and medicine, and he combines the three through his true passion, which is early forensic science. Having been a police detective in my former life, I landed in exactly the right place, and after seven months here, I have turned in my mop and duster to take my full-time position as Gray's assistant.

My current concern has nothing to do with murder or forensics. It's the first of December, and I am tired of waiting for someone to discuss the upcoming holidays. So I'm taking the initiative, having cornered both Gray and Isla in the library.

KELLEY ARMSTRONG

Gray is reading the newspaper, and his sister is at the desk, editing the account of our latest adventure. Both look up at my pronouncement.

"It's time to discuss Christmas," I say again.

Gray shakes out the paper. "I cannot believe you would say such a thing, Mallory. You, a representative of the law, suggesting we discuss *Christmas?*"

I arch one brow.

"That is—" He lowers his voice. "—illegal."

I roll my eyes. "It's December first. The official date on which we can start playing Christmas carols, wrapping presents, hanging decorations…"

"Illegal. All of it."

I eye him. "Is this your way of saying you don't celebrate? That's fine. Just say so."

"Do we celebrate Christmas, Isla?" Gray asks.

His sister's blue eyes widen in mock horror. "Certainly not. It's illegal."

"Banned," Gray says, folding his paper and setting it aside. "And in this household, we follow the rules."

I snort at that. "Follow the *law*, yes. You most certainly do not follow the rules. Either of you. If you want to pull a prank on the time traveler, please try something more believable than saying Christmas is…"

I slow. Even as I say the words, a childhood memory surfaces, my nan saying something about Christmas not being a holiday when she was a child. Her eyes had been sparkling when she said it, which meant I presumed it was one of those "back in my day"

SCHEMES & SCANDALS

tall tales, like my Canadian grandparents who insisted they'd walked five miles to school each day. Uphill. Both ways.

"Wait," I say. "This *is* a joke, right?"

"Hardly. The mere mention of Christmas can still get you hanged in Scotland."

"Duncan…" Isla says. "If you expect to convince her you are serious, you cannot make the tale utterly outlandish." She looks at me. "Yes, it *was* banned, at one time. While it no longer is, it is still not commonly celebrated."

"Christmas was…banned?"

"In Scotland."

I peer at her, still not sure this isn't a joke. "What happened?"

"The Reformation. Christmas was considered both a pagan celebration and a Catholic one, which was practically the same thing. The Church of Scotland prohibited the celebration of it."

"What about Hogmanay? That's pagan."

Isla shrugs. "Scots always find a way around such things. Christmas was banned, so we simply moved the pagan traditions of the solstice to Hogmanay, which, being a secular holiday, the Church could do nothing about."

"Clever. So despite the ban being lifted, people still don't celebrate Christmas?"

She sets down her pen. "It is not a public holiday, but it *is* growing in popularity. If it is important to you, we will celebrate."

"No, I'll stick with Hogmanay. I used to celebrate that with my nan. My parents and I would stay in Canada for Christmas with my other grandparents and then come over to spend Hogmanay with Nan."

KELLEY ARMSTRONG

Hogmanay is what the Scots call the last day of the year. In other words, it's New Year's Eve, but a much bigger deal than it is in North America. Of all the traditions, my favorite custom was fireball swinging...which is exactly what it sounds like. You make a ball of flammable material, attach it to a chain, set it alight and swing it over your head. Like an industrial-strength firework sparkler.

"If you *do* want Christmas..." Gray says.

"Nah, I just like the trappings," I say. "The decorations, the parties, the gift giving. I can get that with Hogmanay." I pause. "You guys do celebrate that, right?"

"We most certainly do. And on that note..." He glances at his sister. "Isla? Would you reach into the top left drawer there? I believe you'll find an early holiday gift for you and Mallory."

She finds an envelope bearing Gray's impeccable script and holds it out to me. "Would you like to do the honors?"

I wave for her to go ahead. She opens it and gasps as she takes out what looks like calling cards. Then she peers at her brother.

"Please tell me this is not a joke."

His brows shoot up. "I never joke."

"You just told poor Mallory that she could be hanged for mentioning Christmas."

"Perhaps she could be. The ban may no longer be well enforced, but if they wanted to make an example of someone, Mallory would be a fine choice."

I toss my hair. "They'd never hang me. I'm a pretty girl with blond curls and big blue eyes." I bat those eyes at him. "The public would rise up in howls of outrage."

"Not if they knew you were also a thief."

SCHEMES & SCANDALS

"Former thief. Reformed. And that wasn't even me. It was Catriona."

"Ah, right. You can explain that to them. Tell them that you are actually from the twenty-first century, and they won't hang you for mentioning Christmas. They'll hang you as a witch." He glances at me. "We still do that here."

"Scotland has not hanged witches in a hundred years," Isla says hotly.

"They would make an exception for Mallory."

Isla glares at him and waves the tickets. "So these *are* a prank then?"

Gray sobers and meets her gaze. "Would I honestly do that to you, Isla?"

She inhales sharply. "They're real?"

"Very real."

She stares at him, speechless. I hurry to the desk, read the tickets and let out a squeal of glee.

T WO

I AM GOING to see Charles Dickens. Right now. I am walking along crowded George Street, heading to the Assembly Rooms music hall to see *the* Charles Dickens. When I was in elementary school, my parents snagged tickets to see the Spice Girls, and as happy as I'd been then, I think I'm even more excited now.

My dad is an English prof. I grew up on Dickens. Landing in an era where he's still alive and writing? I'd hardly been able to fathom it.

Many of my favorite classic novelists are still alive in this time. George Eliot. Wilkie Collins. Mary Elizabeth Braddon. I won't have much chance of seeing them—they're busy doing writerly things—but Charles Dickens tours. Or he did. He's now on his farewell circuit. He'd been due to stop in Edinburgh in February, but by the time Isla heard of it, she wasn't able to get tickets. That stop had to be rescheduled, though, because he injured his foot, which had caused such an outcry that the newspaper had to print his doctor's note to prove it.

KELLEY ARMSTRONG

The stop was rescheduled for late December, and that's how Gray obtained tickets for the last performance. Because, while Christmas might not be celebrated in Scotland, some of the wealthy travel to England for the festivities, and he snagged four tickets from an acquaintance who could no longer attend.

Isla and I get two of those tickets. Gray is accompanying us, along with his best friend, Detective Hugh McCreadie.

The music hall is only about a quarter mile from Gray's Robert Street town house, so we are walking. To be honest, we walk most places. I won't say that Victorian Edinburgh is a particularly pleasant place to stroll, given the amount of excrement, not all of it from horses. Add in the amount of precipitation, and you can't even avoid that excrement, because it melts into every puddle. But boots come clean, and these days, I don't even need to clean my own. Coach travel might be cleaner, but we can usually get where we want to go faster on foot. Also, being late December, the precipitation is all snow, which blankets the soot-covered city in white and also freezes the puddles, bodily waste and all.

The music hall, like Gray's town house, is in the New Town. Initially, that's where the wealthy moved to escape the poverty of the Old Town. These days, it's home to both the upper class and the upper-middle, like the Gray family.

We are dressed for a night on the town. Gray wears a silk top hat and a long coat over a black wool three-piece suit with a starched white shirt and silk cravat. McCreadie is, as always, more stylish, with his checked jacket slightly shorter and more fitted, as is the incoming style. Isla has moved far enough from mourning that she's able to wear lilac, and her dress is divine, with silver

SCHEMES & SCANDALS

buttons and silver-gray pinstriping plus wider strips of silver-gray along the bottom of the sleeves and skirts. My own dress is the same one I wore to a party last month: turquoise silk with brown embroidery and beadwork, and brown taffeta trim.

To accommodate the narrow walking path, McCreadie and Isla are ahead of us. Isla has only to slip, one boot barely sliding, before McCreadie has his elbow out for her to take. It's chivalrous, but also an excuse to have Isla on his arm, one she happily accepts. Just as I happily accept Gray's arm when he notices them and puts out his arm for me. It's an old-fashioned way of walking, the man with his elbow extended, the woman holding it. Very Victorian. Also, a welcome bit of human contact in a world where that is just not done.

In this era, physical intimacy is for couples and, even then, only in the bedroom. Even hugs between friends are not a thing, and I find myself missing that and cherishing the moments where I have an excuse to do something like hold Gray's arm.

As we near the theater, we need to merge into a stream of fellow attendees. Though everyone is dressed in their finest, not all of it comes from New Town shops. There are plenty of second- and even third-hand dresses and suits. It's appropriate that a Dickens reading should be accessible to the working class. It would be even better if it were accessible to the *poor*, but that's too much to hope for. Gray said that the stalls are priced at five shillings, which my math skills tell me is about thirty dollars in my own world.

As we draw near the music hall, the jabbering of voices whisks me back to sporting events in Vancouver. It sounds like resellers offering overpriced tickets to a sold-out game, but as I draw close,

KELLEY ARMSTRONG

I realize it's actually the other way around. People are banging on the ticket booth, offering to pay as much as five pounds for those cheap seats, as if the venue might be hiding some in reserve. I also notice that no one is stepping forward to sell *their* tickets for that price.

The commotion, however, means we need to slow with the desperate would-be buyers partly blocking the entrance. McCreadie grumbles about that.

"Someone should have had a few officers assigned for crowd control," I murmur to him. "Pity we don't know anyone who could help them out now."

"Be my guest," McCreadie says. "If I take on that lot, I won't be seeing the performance."

"And so you will not interfere," Isla says, tightening her grip on his arm.

"I will not," he says. "I can still grumble, though."

Slowing means we're stuck standing outside. Being stuck standing outside means people start gawking around the queue. Gazes swing to Gray. That's understandable. He's just over six feet, with broad shoulders and striking—if severe—features. Admittedly, McCreadie is better looking, remarkably handsome even with fashionably thick whiskers. Yet the gazes fall on Gray, and it's not his height that does it. It's his brown skin. He might have been raised by Frances Gray, but his mother was Irvine Gray's mistress, and obviously a woman of color, though Irvine took any details to his grave.

We're in the days of the British Empire, when travel and immigration is easier, if not exactly easy. I can look down the queue

SCHEMES & SCANDALS

and see several people of color. Most, however, are clearly working class. The one young Black woman in a fashionable gown accompanies an older white woman in a manner that suggests she's a companion or lady's maid. I have to crane my neck and squint to see any person of color who looks middle class.

What gets people's attention isn't that Gray is a person of color; it's that he dresses as if he's wealthy enough to have a tailor, which he does. Admittedly, sometimes they also look because he hasn't bothered to change out of a shirt spattered in blood, but that's thankfully not the case today. These days, though, there's another reason people gawk, and that's what I'm on the watch for.

A few months ago, someone started chronicling Gray's adventures in crime solving. Those adventures may have coincided with him taking on a certain assistant, but I'm still blaming poor McCreadie. Between the three of us—and Isla, when a case interests her—we've solved a few murders. The person who interested that writer, though, was Gray. Well, Gray and his pretty assistant, but my role in the stories seems mostly window dressing.

The Mysterious Adventures of the Gray Doctor has recently changed writers and—thankfully—titles. The previous author has been shut down, by methods known only to the new author, who granted Isla a cut plus editorial oversight. There was no way of getting rid of the stories altogether, so taking control of the narrative was our best bet. For now, they're a niche publication, mostly appealing to mothers and their children. Why are women and children the primary market for tales of murder and mayhem? Because these are Victorians.

KELLEY ARMSTRONG

Tonight, while I do see one mother and her children gesturing at us and whispering, they don't approach, so we can pretend all is well and we are safe in our bubble of anonymity.

Soon we're inside the music hall. Our tickets are for the balcony. In the modern world, I like seats in the orchestra, where I can truly appreciate live performances. Here, the orchestra seats are the stalls, and the stalls are for those who can't afford better. My disappointment evaporates when I *see* those stalls. Most of the seats are on church-like pews, with hundreds of people jammed into an area that defies any sort of safety code. One scream of "Fire!" and dozens would be trampled. I decide I'm fine with the balcony.

We aren't in actual balconies, either. More like having seats in concert stands. McCreadie goes down the aisle first, followed by Isla, followed by me and then Gray. While Isla and I would have chosen to sit beside each other anyway, this arrangement is natural for the time period—the men flanking the women so they don't need to sit beside strangers who might be male.

We settle in, and we all remove our hats, which is expected and even mentioned on the tickets. As we wait, Isla and I discuss Dickens's latest work, *No Thoroughfare*, which he wrote in collaboration with Wilkie Collins. Isla has seen the show. I have not, though I read the novel form in the twenty-first century.

"I hear he is working on a new book," Isla says. "I am hoping he will discuss it tonight." She wags her finger at me. "And no spoilers from you."

Which novel would that be? Admittedly, I'm not great with dates. I know Dickens's work but not the order or years of publication. I think back to the library at the town house. Which book is

SCHEMES & SCANDALS

missing? I'm still working through that when someone steps on the stage to announce the main event.

The music hall venue is appropriate, because this feels much more like a concert than an author reading. I can't hear what the MC is saying, as people keep chattering and others keep shushing them, often louder than the actual talkers. Finally, I catch the tail end of the MC's speech.

"—will begin with a seasonal reading of *A Christmas Carol*."

I look at Gray and arch one brow, and there must be accusation in my eyes because he leans over and whispers, "The poor man will be hanged for certain now. Such a loss to the literary world."

It's the week after Christmas, and while there *were* some shop and house decorations, overall, it was far less than I'd expected. I know from my father that the Victorian era was the time when Christmas was still becoming the spectacle it is in the modern world. Credit—blame?—for that can be laid, at least in part, at the feet of the man about to mount the stage and the story he is about to read.

In North America, a secular Christmas revolves around the family, especially children. You get together with your nearest and dearest, and you make a magical day for the little ones in your life. You also share your bounty with the less fortunate—'tis the season to be charitable. All that comes from *A Christmas Carol*, which refocused a community-based celebration on the family, especially the children, as well as shining a spotlight on the plight of the poor and the obligations of the wealthy.

Isla had asked whether there was any particular part of Christmas I longed to celebrate. I said no, Hogmanay would do

KELLEY ARMSTRONG

the trick well enough, but I did wake to a plate of sugarplums on Christmas morning. May I also say that, like Turkish delight, sugarplums are not at all what I expected? There's no actual plum involved. It's more like a jawbreaker, with a seed at the center and then layers of sugar. Disappointing, but not nearly on the scale of the Turkish delight debacle. I swear I can still taste the cloying rosewater from *that*.

On the stage, the MC is walking away, and I realize the man standing there now...

It's Charles Dickens.

This is the Dickens I know from photos, mostly taken in this era, showing a man with kind eyes, balding hair, and a somewhat unkempt long beard. In those photographs, though, he's always dead somber, and that is not the man I see before me. He is smiling and animated and moves spryly to center stage.

As Dickens begins, I ease back in my seat, prepared for a relaxing literary performance. I've attended readings of *A Christmas Carol* before. I even participated in a group reading for one of my dad's university classes. Being the only child among the actors, you can guess who I played. God bless us every one.

Although that had been a reading rather than a dramatization, I'd treated it like a full-blown performance, limping around the stage and looking pathetic but hopeful as only Tiny Tim can. I had, in short, hammed it up...and as Dickens begins to read on stage, I realize I might have underplayed it.

When Isla said it would be a two-hour performance, I'd been confused. I've been to author readings. The best are short and sweet. Even the longest top out at thirty minutes, which let me

SCHEMES & SCANDALS

tell you, is a long time to be actively listening to someone who is not an actor or a public speaker. No matter how interesting the material, most authors are not meant to read their work.

Dickens is an exception, I think. Possibly because, at one time, he'd entertained thoughts of acting as a career path. As I watch, I'm honestly not sure what I think. My preconceptions are smashed to such splinters that I can only sit there and gape.

In my time, Dickens is classic literature. I know that was very different during his own life. He was considered a populist writer, with all the scorn that can bring. His appeal went far beyond the educated upper—or even middle—class. He told stories about the poor and working classes. Real Victorian life, the sort I see every time I visit the Old Town.

Yet as much as I understood his broad class appeal, I couldn't help but still stick him in the "classic author" box, alongside the other literary greats. Which means I am in no way prepared for what I am witnessing.

This is Dickens's final tour because the performances are getting to be too much for him, physically. Yet the man I see is in his fifties and hardly doddering. The reason these performances exhaust him? Because they're actual performances.

I am treated—if that's the word—to the most gonzo reading of *A Christmas Carol* ever. It's as if seven-year-old Mallory got to play all the parts and played her little unselfconscious heart out. Except the guy doing the performance is Charles Dickens himself.

"What do you think?" Isla whispers. "Are readings like this in your day?"

KELLEY ARMSTRONG

I try to imagine Margaret Atwood getting up on stage and doing this sort of "reading" from *The Handmaid's Tale*.

Nope.

I can't imagine even the most populist authors of my time giving a performance like this.

And this is Charles freaking Dickens.

"He's very…energetic," I say.

"Isn't he? They say his readings bring him more income than his books do."

"I…can imagine."

As I watch, I am reminded again how much this world is not what I expected. When I silence my preconceptions, I begin to enjoy it, rather than staring like an elderly aunt at her first rave.

Dickens finishes his reading from *A Christmas Carol*. Then it's on to *Oliver Twist*. Good choice. Definitely a crowd-pleaser. I'm wondering what scene he'll read when—

It's the Nancy and Sikes scene. The brutal murder of Nancy at the hands of her boyfriend, Bill Sikes. I glance around nervously. This is an all-ages crowd, and he's reading what might be the most violent scene of his career. And everyone in the music hall—from children to well-dressed ladies—hangs on his every word.

"This is…" I manage to choke out, "an interesting choice."

"He always reads this one," Isla says. "The crowd would rise up in protest if he did not."

I sit there, watching a packed theater of prim Victorians devouring Charles Dickens's reading of a gruesome and tragic murder scene.

"At least a dozen women will faint," Isla whispers. "Loudly and enthusiastically."

SCHEMES & SCANDALS

I stare at her. Then I stare at the bloodthirsty crowd of ladies and gentlemen, all of them dressed in infinite layers as protection against the horror and shame of revealing a stray bit of bare skin.

I will *never* understand Victorians.

"Not what you expected?" Gray whispers at my ear.

I turn and gesticulate, unable to put my thoughts into words. His lips curve in a smile that grows until he needs to cough in his hand, politely, before he laughs aloud. Then I settle in to watch the reading…while Gray settles in for, I suspect, the even more entertaining spectacle of watching *me* watching the reading.

Three

THE PERFORMANCE is over, and I've realized I'm not getting my book signed. I'd tracked down a first edition of *Our Mutual Friend*, my favorite Dickens novel, and tucked it into my bag. The readings I've attended always culminate in a signing. But, again, the author events I've attended aren't two hours of a performance so energetic that I'm exhausted from just watching.

Isla and McCreadie are gone. McCreadie had scoped out a suitable spot to enjoy a polite tipple after the show, and we'd encouraged them to escape as quickly as possible and snag a table. Any chance Gray and I get to give McCreadie and Isla time together is a chance we take.

Gray and I have lingered, with me clutching my book and looking around hopefully, as if there's a hidden "author signing" for those in the know.

"You brought a book?" Gray says.

My cheeks heat. "I was hoping to get it signed, but I'm guessing that's not a thing."

KELLEY ARMSTRONG

"I have seen signed books. I even purchased several for Isla. But they came that way at the shop."

I try not to look disappointed. "Got it. And after that performance, I can't imagine he'd want to sign hundreds of books."

"Perhaps..." Gray looks about and puts a hand to my back. "Let us go this way. There's a corridor into the back rooms where Mr. Dickens would be."

I dig in my heels against his steering. "I'm not waylaying him while he's resting after his performance."

"No, but if we are down there, and he happens to walk out, and he happens to notice a young woman clutching one of his books and looking very hopeful..."

I should refuse. Especially since, if I do catch Dickens's eye, it won't be because of the book. I look like a cross between a milk-maid and a young Marilyn Monroe, all bold curves and blond curls. I've finally begun to accept that this is me now. My body, not that of a cold-blooded thief named Catriona Mitchell. But I still hate using this body to my advantage. Well, unless I'm solving a case. Then all bets are off.

Even as I inwardly balk, though, my knees unlock, and I let Gray steer me. I tell myself I'm giving Isla more time with McCreadie. Am I also giving myself more time with Gray? Of course not. I see him every day. We spend hours working together. Okay, yes, holding cadavers and taking notes isn't the same as a social outing, but still...

Our relationship is a professional one with a personal angle, that angle being friendship. If part of me has started hoping for more, well, that's on me. Gray has given no sign that he feels the same. Which is fine. That'd be far too complicated.

26

SCHEMES & SCANDALS

Gray leads me through a door and then down a few stairs and along a hall. It feels as if we're about to enter the bowels of the Assembly Rooms, but instead, we come out into a small reception area with at least twenty people milling about chatting and enjoying glasses of wine. Gray straightens, pulling on his upper-crust airs.

He steers me through with that gentle hand, his fingertips barely touching my back. As we pass a table, he deftly plucks two glasses from it. He hands me one, and we settle into a corner, where he positions himself with his back to the other guests and his front blocking me, to keep them from looking at us too closely.

"Let us eavesdrop a bit," he murmurs. "See whether there is any indication that these fine people expect the illustrious author to join us."

I nod, sip at my drink, and try not to make a face. I thought it was wine. It's not.

"Port," Gray says. "Poor Mallory."

Port is not to my taste. It's another thing, like sugarplums, that I only read about in Regency and Victorian novels, where it sounded delightful. Dinner ends, and you all retire with glasses of port. Yes, I know it still exists in my time, but I'd never tried it, so I didn't realize it's just overly sweet wine.

Gray opens his mouth to say something else, when a voice says, "Duncan?"

The familiarity of the address has me looking up sharply. First names are for family and close acquaintances. I'm still working on calling him "Duncan," as if I've absorbed the culture. So hearing someone call him that in public is the first thing that gets my

KELLEY ARMSTRONG

attention. The second is the way his head jerks up. Distress flickers over his face.

"Dr. Duncan Gray." The woman's voice grows closer now, though I still can't see her with Gray blocking my view. Then he slowly turns.

The woman is older than us—maybe in her late thirties. She's gorgeous, with raven-black hair, perfectly cut features, and bright blue eyes. Her brilliant green dress makes me feel as if I'm still wearing my drab day gown.

It might seem as if it'd be wonderful to wake up a decade younger, but it's awkward in many ways, and this is one of them— where I feel the gaze of someone older sweep past and dismiss me as a mere girl.

"This is not where I expected to find you, Duncan," the woman says as her fingertips tap his jacket sleeve. "You have developed a taste for literary culture?"

"I read," he says, a little tersely. "But I am here with my sister Isla, who is a great admirer of Mr. Dickens's work. As is Miss Mitchell here."

The woman's gaze flicks over me again, and she gives Gray a look I can't quite read. Should I slip away and let them talk? Or is that the last thing Gray wants? I can't tell.

I give him the choice by murmuring, "I'm going to set down this port, Dr. Gray. It is not quite to my taste."

He doesn't argue, and I make my way toward the nearest table. I can still hear them behind me.

"I heard you hired a young woman for an assistant," the woman says. "A former maid. I take it that is her."

SCHEMES & SCANDALS

"Yes."

The woman sighs. "Oh, Duncan. I ignored the titters and insinuations, and I commended you for being so open-minded. I know you had a terrible time finding assistants, and I was glad you had located one. But... Really, Duncan? I expected better of you."

"Miss Mitchell *is* my assistant."

He grinds out the words, and I set down my drink.

"My apologies, ma'am," I say when I reach them. "I realized I did not introduce myself. I am Mallory Mitchell, Dr. Gray's assistant."

Her gaze flicks to Gray, waiting for him to introduce her, as is proper. Instead, he stands there, with a look that wonders whether he can skip this part.

Just introduce us, Gray, and we can make our excuses—

"This is Lady Patricia Inglis," Gray says, and if I still had the port glass, I might have dropped it.

I school my features fast and give the slightest curtsy, hoping nothing in my face reveals my dismay.

There's a reason Lady Inglis uses Gray's first name and acts as if she knows him well. She does. In the biblical sense even.

When I first arrived in this time period, I found a letter in Catriona's dresser. A letter from Lady Inglis to Gray, one that Catriona had apparently intercepted before he received it. She'd likely been looking for blackmail material, maybe suspecting it was from a lover. What she got was even better. Not a sweet love note from a paramour but a full-on intimate missive, in which Lady Inglis had tried to tempt Gray back to her bed by reminding him how much fun he'd had there. Super awkward, and as soon as I figured out what it was, I'd stopped reading.

29

KELLEY ARMSTRONG

Even more awkward? The fact that just last month I confessed to him about the letter. I'd felt honor-bound to tell him Catriona stole it, but it was a very uncomfortable conversation. He'd told me to destroy it, which I had.

So this beautiful and elegant woman is Lady Inglis? Of course she is, because that's what I've pictured as the sort of woman Gray would be with. Mature, possibly even older, but gorgeous and refined, educated and charming. Okay, I haven't seen the charming part yet, but I'm sure she is, when she's not wondering what the hell her former lover is doing messing around with a girl barely out of her teens.

"Did you enjoy the performance, ma'am?" I ask.

"I did." Her gaze goes to the book I'm still clutching. "Is that one of Mr. Dickens's works?"

"*Our Mutual Friend*," I say. "My favorite. I have never been to this sort of event, and I was hoping for a signature, but obviously, that is not done." I give a rueful smile. "Dr. Gray? If you like, I could go join Mrs. Ballantyne and Mr. McCreadie."

"Certainly not," he says. "It is dark outside. I must accompany you." He turns to Lady Inglis. "But Miss Mitchell is correct that my sister is waiting for us." He tips his top hat. "Good evening to you, Lady Inglis."

As we turn away, she says, "I could ask Mr. Dickens to sign that book for you, Miss Mitchell. He knows my parents from years back."

I don't hesitate. I know this for what it is—grabbing back Gray's attention with an underhanded ploy. By the way Gray tenses, he also knows what it is. And yet...

SCHEMES & SCANDALS

The reason it's truly underhanded? She's not offering something *he* wants. She's offering something his companion wants, and she must know Gray well enough to realize he can't walk away from that.

"I'm fine," I murmur under my breath. "I don't need—"

"I am sorry to interfere with your evening out," Lady Inglis says. "But I have been wanting to talk to you, Duncan."

His cheek twitches, but before he can comment, she hurries on with, "A business matter. I was trying to determine how best to bring it to your attention. I suspected a—" She clears her throat softly. "—a letter would not do. Nor a message asking to meet with you. Yet I did not wish to show up at your house."

"If you need something, Lady Inglis," he says coolly, "then I would appreciate you saying so and not tacking on an offer to help Miss Mitchell."

"I *can* help her, though. I can get that signature. As for what I need… I wish to hire you as a detective."

A beat pause before Gray straightens. "Then you have come to the wrong person. I am a scientist. Any matter of detection would go to the police. I could ask Hugh to speak to you."

Gray is being disingenuous here. He may not be a police detective, but he has come to call himself, only half-jokingly, a consulting detective. Yes, that's my fault, and I owe Sir Arthur Conan Doyle for making the offhand reference that Gray liked enough to adopt.

Unlike Sherlock Holmes, though, Gray does not hire out his services. He only works for the police, specifically with McCreadie, and he takes no compensation. I could—and do—grumble at that,

KELLEY ARMSTRONG

but I also know how little Victorian police officers make, and the department needs the money more than Gray does.

"I know you do more than work in your laboratory these days, Duncan," Lady Inglis says.

"Does your case involve a dead body?"

"Heavens, no."

"Then I cannot help you. Farewell, Lady—"

"Duncan, please." She reaches for his arm and then stops herself. "I understand you are suspicious of my motives, which is why I could not determine the best way to bring this to you. I made…"

Her gaze darts my way, and she clears her throat. "My previous attempts at communication were rebuffed, and I accepted that you did not wish to see me again. It is not as if I have hounded you, Duncan. I made two attempts, and then I stopped. Please do not insult me by presuming that is what I am doing. I think you know me better than that."

"I do, and I did not mean to insinuate anything. I am stating a fact. I am not a detective for hire. I am a scientist who occasionally works with the police in matters regarding murder."

"Blackmail," she blurts. Then she quickly glances around and lowers her voice. "I am being blackmailed, Duncan, and it is not a matter I can take to the police. Nor is it one I would take to a stranger. I am a respected widow, and what I am being threatened with…" She plucks nervously at her cameo choker. "It is very personal."

Gray's voice lowers, touched with the first hint of compassion. "I understand, Patricia, but this really is not my area of expertise."

SCHEMES & SCANDALS

"Could you at least hear me out?" Her gaze moves to me. "Both of you. I understand Miss Mitchell is your assistant, and she would therefore be involved in any detection you might do."

I grant her a point for that. She's making it clear that this isn't about getting Gray's attention. Which means she really is being blackmailed.

Gray's gaze cuts to me.

"Our schedule is not overly occupied, sir," I murmur.

"We will hear you out," Gray says to Lady Inglis. "I presume we cannot do that here?"

She shakes her head. "It is very private, as I said. I would invite you both to lunch with me tomorrow if that is amenable."

"It is," Gray says. "Now, as for that signature…"

"It's fine," I say quickly.

"I can do better than a signature," Lady Inglis says with a soft smile.

She leads us into a side hall. Partway down it, she stops and knocks.

A man opens the door, but from our angle, I can only hear the voice.

"Patsy!" he says. "I had hoped I might see you while I am in town. I am having dinner with your parents tomorrow."

"And I shall be there," she says. "May we step in? I have a young woman who is most eager to meet you."

Dickens waves us forward, Gray nudges me, and I find myself standing in front of Charles Dickens.

Four

E'RE QUICKLY ushered inside before anyone hears Dickens speaking. Apparently, that reception room isn't actually a reception. It's a place for the wealthy attendees to sip port while the rabble clears out. Meanwhile, Dickens is staying in his room waiting for *that* rabble to clear out.

Lady Inglis excuses herself with an invitation to join her for lunch the next day. And then I am left standing in front of Charles Dickens, gaping, with Gray tucked in behind, ceding the stage to me.

"Sir," I say, words jumbling as they spill out. "Mr. Dickens. It is an honor. I… I am a great admirer of your work, and I…"

I babble sentiments he has heard a million times as my brain screams for me to do better. I am meeting *Charles Dickens*. I have the chance to speak to an author whose work helped shape my literary childhood. An author who died a century before I was born.

Say something, damn it.

Say something *meaningful*.

KELLEY ARMSTRONG

I clutch the book to my chest, as if that will steady my nerves. "I appreciate all you have done to tell the stories of those who do not normally get them, the insight you give into the lives of the poor and working classes."

He blinks. Am I not supposed to say that? I remember that he has been mocked for "plumbing the depths" by contemporaries who only tell the stories of the privileged.

"All lives are worthy of note," I say. "And the lives of the rich fill enough books."

He smiles at that. "They do indeed."

I continue, warming to my subject. "Too often, when we look back, we see only those whom history deemed worthy. When we lose the stories of the majority, we lose history itself. We see our past through such a narrow lens that we cannot truly understand what it was like to live in such a time, and I appreciate what you have done to widen that lens for future readers."

His gaze goes from Gray to me. Do I sound as if I am parroting Gray's words? Do I look as if these thoughts cannot possibly be my own? Sadly, yes, I do.

"Miss Mitchell has many opinions," Gray says. "On many topics."

"So I see." Dickens inclines his head my way. "Thank you. That is very insightful and very satisfying to hear."

"Your stories will provide insight and entertainment for generations to come," I say. "Long after some of your contemporaries are relegated to the dust bin—or to required reading for higher learning—people will continue to read and enjoy your work. I am certain of it."

SCHEMES & SCANDALS

He smiles. "From your lips to God's ear."

When I fall silent, not wanting to speechify, Gray murmurs, "Miss Mitchell has a book she would like you to sign, if we could impose."

"Certainly." Dickens reaches out, and I hand it to him. When he sees which one it is, his brows rise. "You enjoyed this?"

I manage to find my smile. "It is my favorite. I know, I just spoke of the lives of the poor, and this is not that sort of book, but it has my favorite female character of yours."

"Bella Wilfer?"

"Yes. Also, the story is a mystery, and I am overly fond of mysteries."

His smile grows. "One can never be too fond of mysteries. That is what my next novel will be. An unabashed mystery."

He takes the book to a side table with a pen and ink. "Inscribed to Miss Mitchell?"

"Mallory Mitchell, please." I shift closer. "About your next book. My friend—Dr. Gray's sister—was dearly hoping you'd discuss it during the performance. She will be devastated to have missed meeting you. Is there any chance I might take her a hint or two about the next book, in recompense?"

"Certainly." He finishes signing and leaves the book open to dry. "Beware, though, that I may tell more than you wish to know. No project is as exciting to an author as the one they are currently working on. It is bright and shiny, and no critic has read it to tell them where it is dull and tarnished."

I laugh softly. "I will take whatever you care to provide, Mr. Dickens."

"Then may I offer you both a drink?"

He lifts a bottle of what looks like imported Italian wine. We both accept, and Dickens begins to pour.

"My next book is, as I said, a mystery," he begins. "It tells the tale of a man who disappears, an orphan named…"

I know the answer before he gives it, and with that name, my heart thuds into my boots.

"Edwin Drood."

I SPEND THE next hour talking to a dead man.

I know it is wrong to say that, to even think it, but I can't help myself. When Dickens tells me what he's writing, I know what it means.

That within a year, he will be dead.

I said I was no good with dates, and here's the proof. My focus was always on Dickens's work rather than the man himself. If asked, I'd have guessed he died when he was elderly. Certainly not in his fifties. Certainly not after I just saw him tearing up the stage in that performance.

I recall that he dies of a stroke. That is all. And dying of a stroke means it's not as if I could say, "Beware the Ides of March… and back-clapping friends." He will die, and there's nothing I can do about that.

I spend an hour listening to Dickens discuss *The Mystery of Edwin Drood*. A book he will never finish. A story the world has been trying to finish for him ever since.

SCHEMES & SCANDALS

I don't sit there in stunned silence. That would be unforgivably rude. I have a chance to listen to Charles Dickens talk about his work, not from a stage, but in person. Once I am past the shock and those premature stabs of grief, I am the best audience he could want. That is what I can give him...and so I do.

THE NEXT DAY. Gray and I set off to lunch at Lady Inglis's house. I'm wearing my day dress—much simpler than my gown the night before but still a "going out" dress. To accommodate the winter weather, I have fur-lined boots, a fur-lined muff, a fur-lined hat, and fur-lined gloves. I don't even want to calculate the number of tiny creatures that died to keep me warm. In my world, I'd never have worn any of this, but synthetics aren't a thing, so my options are fur or "wrap my feet in newspaper before putting them in my boots." To be honest, I did try that, and it's as uncomfortable as it sounds, but I might have continued doing it if Gray and Isla hadn't been horrified and tried to buy me velvet to wrap my feet instead. And so this was another point where I had to concede my twenty-first-century ethics really only worked for the twenty-first century. My concession is that all my outerwear is second-hand. The critters were already dead, and I'm extending their afterlife.

For my jacket... Well, I don't have one. I have a cloak. While I have seen a few women in winter coats, cloaks work better over dresses, especially now that the bustle is coming into style. And, yes, the cloak has fur, damn it.

KELLEY ARMSTRONG

Despite all my dress layers and fur-lined outerwear, we aren't walking to lunch. Lady Inglis lives outside town in a country estate, one of those places that will someday be a fancy historic house considered part of Edinburgh...if it isn't sold and torn down for a new housing development.

I can be outraged at the thought of losing such historic homes, but I often wonder whether that's the New World citizen in me. I grew up in a city where the oldest surviving building only dates back to the decade I currently inhabit. I want to preserve *everything*. But these old houses don't have any true historic value. They're just homes, and there are cities full of them. Also, they weren't built for twenty-first-century living, and retrofitting them isn't always an option.

Given Lady Inglis's title, presumably her late husband was a viscount, baron or some such. Their house reflects that. It's not the monstrosity Gray's sister Annis lived in with her earl husband. It's more like something I'd picture in a Jane Austen novel. A tidy house in the country with a bit of land.

As we approach, I glance at Gray, ramrod straight on the opposite coach seat.

"If you don't want to do this, we can turn around now," I say. "She won't have spotted us."

"It is fine."

I sigh. "You've been saying that since last night, and it doesn't get any more convincing with practice. I regret getting that signature—"

"Nonsense. I am glad you got it, and I am the one who insisted on meeting Mr. Dickens. You tried to demur."

SCHEMES & SCANDALS

"But if it feels like you owe her, you don't. I can handle this on my own. I *am* your assistant, after all. I can take the meeting and say you were called away on an emergency."

"An undertaker emergency?"

"Hey, it can happen. Lady Inglis doesn't need an explanation. I can write down the details, and if I want to investigate, I can. On my own. *I'm* the professional detective, after all."

"If I seem out of sorts, it has nothing to do with the possibility of helping Lady Inglis. She is being blackmailed and cannot go to the police, and so she deserves help."

"Does she?" I meet his gaze. "I'm trying not to pry here, Duncan, but I'll admit I've been hoping you'd give me more on your own. I don't need details. I just need to know if she…"

If she hurt you. If she did anything that means I don't want to help her.

"If I need to be wary," I say.

"Of Patricia?" He stops, and his lips purse, as if he didn't mean to be so informal. "Not at all. She is a good woman, deserving of our help."

Which doesn't really answer my question. Lady Inglis can be a decent person and still have hurt him. Yes, I know *he* ended the relationship, but that doesn't mean she didn't do something to deserve it.

"Fine, I'll drop it," I mutter, less graciously than I'd like. The coach has pulled up to the house anyway. Too late to turn back. When it stops, I move toward the door.

"This is very uncomfortable for me," Gray says.

"Which is why I suggested you stay behind."

KELLEY ARMSTRONG

According to the dictates of polite society, Gray should disembark first, to help me down. Sometimes he does, but he's just as likely to forget, lost in his own thoughts.

Today, when Simon—our groom—opens the door, Gray waves him back to the driver's seat. Then he pulls the door shut.

"Lady Inglis and I had a...somewhat humiliating misunderstanding," he says. "When I...am seeing a woman, I expect that I am the only person she is seeing, as she will be the only one I am seeing. I made the mistake of not being explicit about that."

"Ah."

"It was not my finest moment," he says. "The fault was my own, for presuming the relationship was exclusive. I handled it poorly."

"But she *did* try to win you back."

He mumbles something I don't catch, and my heart sinks even as I curse myself for that. I'd been under the impression that he'd lost interest or decided the relationship wasn't working. That's not the case and...

Shit.

I was trying to get past the awkwardness of taking a job from Gray's former lover, and now I discover that their breakup wasn't as clear cut as I thought. He hadn't simply moved on. He'd been hurt and retreated and then been too embarrassed to reconcile. I'm caught in between Gray and a former lover he might very well still be interested in.

"I could go," I blurt.

He startles and blinks at me. "What?"

"I could leave. Let you handle this. If you'd...prefer."

His brows knit. "Prefer what?"

SCHEMES & SCANDALS

"To do this on your own. If it is uncomfortable for you, and you are determined to do it, would it be better if I were not there?"

"No, this is fine," he says, and climbs out and walks toward the house without another word.

Five

AS THE butler leads us through the house, I don't notice any of it. I'm too busy fuming at Gray. I've done backflips to be sensitive and suggest ways to alleviate his discomfort, and in the end, all I got was his wasp sting of annoyance.

Screw that, then. He's an adult, and he can make his own choices and deal with his own discomfort. Whatever's going on here is between him and Lady Inglis. I just happen to be stuck in the middle of it.

As long as I'm there, I'll take my place at that center. I'm the detective, and since there are no dead bodies involved, I'm in charge.

We enter the dining room to find Lady Inglis arranging flowers on the side table. That gives me pause. Oh, flower arranging is a very suitable hobby for a wealthy woman. But this is also the era when people assigned meanings to every flower and color. It was a method of communication, especially between men and women. I know nothing about the language of flowers, though I

KELLEY ARMSTRONG

am aware that there could be some meaning in the arrangement Gray might comprehend.

And then I remind myself that I don't give a shit.

I don't even look Gray's way to see his reaction. I greet Lady Inglis and compliment her on the lovely arrangements and the lovely home. She seems startled, and I presume the impression I gave last night was one of slightly less poise.

The flowers are lovely—white honeysuckle and blue cornflowers. The dining room is also lovely, tastefully appointed in the same colors, white and blue, carried from the carpet to the lampshades to the wallpaper.

Lady Inglis invites us to sit at the table, fully set for lunch. She takes what I presume is her usual spot at one end. Gray gets the other, and I'm in the middle, literally this time.

There is a bit of awkward small talk, which I stay out of. Having decided I don't give a damn also means I don't feel the need to smooth the way for Gray. I spend my time discreetly taking in my surroundings.

Most of the art is landscape, but there's a portrait that seems to be Lady Inglis and her father until I realize she's in a wedding gown and he doesn't quite look old enough to be giving away the bride. Her husband, then. In it, Lady Inglis is about twenty. She's holding her new husband's arm, and she doesn't look frightened or even determined. She looks happy. Genuinely glowing.

The first course arrives. At home, lunch is a fairly simple affair, betraying the Grays' middle-class background. There is rarely a first course, and the meal often makes use of leftovers from the day before. That's not frugality as much as convenience and efficiency.

SCHEMES & SCANDALS

Dinner takes much longer to prepare in this period, and unless you have a dedicated cook, shortcuts are essential. One thing we always have, though, is dessert, because our gorgon housekeeper, Mrs. Wallace, dotes on Gray. God forbid the man miss an opportunity to have a rich pastry or slice of cake.

The first course here is a cream of asparagus soup along with fresh bread. I wait for everyone to take their first sips of the soup, and then I say, "You will forgive my bluntness, Lady Inglis, but I do not wish to take up too much of your time. May we discuss the case over lunch?"

Her gaze shoots to Gray, who scoops another spoonful of soup and says, "Miss Mitchell will take the lead here," without looking up.

"Lacking Dr. Gray's background and position, I am usually forgiven for also lacking his manners." I smile, but it feels a little feral. "I am, as I said, rather blunt. I can get to the heart of the matter where he might need to dance around it, and I can ask questions that might give him pause."

"I see," Lady Inglis murmurs. "All right, then. Let us move directly into discussing the situation. As I said, I am being blackmailed. You are aware that I am a widow?"

"I am."

"You said that your background allows you certain liberties. My status allows me others. One is that I do not need to forsake the company of men."

Her gaze holds mine, as if trying to convey a delicate secret that I might be too young to comprehend. Victorians have a reputation for prudery that is well earned. Sex is not a thing you

KELLEY ARMSTRONG

discuss, at least not if you are female…or a male in mixed company. I'm going to presume men talk about it among themselves, but not being a man, I can't comment on that.

I know women—at least those in lower classes—talk about it. But well-to-do ladies do not. This does not mean well-to-do ladies aren't having sex. It doesn't mean that men who turn bright red at the most obtuse mention are not having sex. There is plenty of that going on—and plenty of it is extramarital—but everyone acts as if there isn't, even if they're having it themselves.

I'm sure many widows enjoy their freedom to some extent. God knows, I wish Isla would. But Lady Inglis watches my reaction as if I would be scandalized.

"I understand," I say.

She hesitates. "I am not certain you do. This is a matter of great delicacy, Miss Mitchell."

"You have lovers, and this blackmail is connected to them."

I shouldn't be so blunt. The fact that I am might prove I'm still annoyed with Gray and in a bit of a mood. Her gaze shoots to him, and I notice he gives the barest shake of his head. Telling her that this information did not come from him. Technically true.

I continue, "You forget that I do not share Dr. Gray's background, and certainly not your own, Lady Inglis. These things are much more common—even natural—where I am from."

Catriona actually seemed to be from a middle-class family, but Lady Inglis nods her understanding, even as color touches her cheeks.

The door opens with the second course—lamb cutlets, roasted potatoes, and green beans—and I wait for that to be served and for everyone to take a few bites.

SCHEMES & SCANDALS

"Can you explain the nature of the blackmail?" I say. "Does it come from a former lover?"

"Certainly not." She sets her fork down with a decisive clink. "I am very careful, Miss Mitchell. I would not associate with any man who might do such a thing."

"And you know that because…?"

She blinks, as if taken aback by the very question. "Because they are men of honor."

"If you mean that they are wealthy—"

"That hardly makes them honorable," she says archly. "In fact, in my experience, most dishonorable men come from my own class. I say they are honorable because they choose the companionship of widows over…other options."

"Serving maids and sex workers?"

Lady Inglis chokes on her cutlet, and Gray makes the smallest noise of warning.

"This is why I take charge," I say. "Dr. Gray doesn't even like *hearing* me ask these questions. He certainly wouldn't ask himself. You say your lovers are honorable because they choose mature, unattached women rather than seducing young ones." I pause. "I probably shouldn't include sex workers in that. A fair and respectful exchange is always better than seducing serving maids."

Lady Inglis only stares. Not at me, but at Gray. Rather like Dickens did last night.

"Miss Mitchell has strong opinions," he murmurs, "and no difficulty voicing them."

"If that makes you uncomfortable, I'll stop," I say.

KELLEY ARMSTRONG

"No, it is just…unexpected. You are…very young, and I did not expect…" She manages a smile. "Although, I suppose, if Duncan hired you as his assistant, I should have known you'd be more than you seemed."

"She is," Gray murmurs.

I decide to set aside the question of honorable men for now. From what I understand, Gray's lovers are usually widows, and I agree that is preferable to other options in this world. Sex work is often the course of desperation—and the source of venereal disease. Unmarried women of his own class likely know nothing about the art of preventing pregnancy. And while sex between men and their household staff is common, it's the most problematic of the options.

Whether choosing widows is "honorable" or not, it has nothing to do with whether a man wouldn't blackmail a past lover. My experience—as both a woman and a cop—tells me to be very careful presuming a lover would never blackmail you because once you've left them, they can become a very different person. At sixteen, I made the boneheaded mistake of sending a risqué picture to a boy. I thought I was being sexy—and clever—sending a shot where I was clearly naked but all the "naughty bits" were hidden. Also, he was the sweetest guy, one who would absolutely *never* send it to his friends when I broke up with him.

Lesson learned.

Still, this is not a point I can argue. I've had friends swear up and down that it's safe to send nude pics to their boyfriends, and I've had boyfriends who were offended that I wouldn't send them

SCHEMES & SCANDALS

nude pics. So I'm not fighting Lady Inglis on this. I just know what I know.

"Can you explain the nature of the blackmail?" I say after a few bites of the cutlet, which is really very good.

"Letters of an intimate nature," she says, and I nearly choke on my mouthful.

I manage to swallow and dab my napkin at my lips to hide my reaction.

"Letters you had sent to a former lover?" I say as evenly as I can.

"No."

I look up at her.

She continues, "I sent them to someone I have been involved with for many years. He was a dear friend of my husband and became my friend as well. After my husband passed…" Her cheeks color, just a bit. "Eventually, we grew closer."

"I understand."

"It did not happen while my husband was alive," she says firmly. "Nor even shortly after his death. I did not have such feelings for this friend until significantly later. But since then, our friendship is periodically…more intimate."

Friends with benefits, Victorian-style? That actually surprises me. Not the sex part but the friendship part. Friendship between men and women isn't common in this time. It *can't* be common in a world where women are guarded as if any man who is alone with them for five minutes will have them against the nearest wall.

Gray and I fight that battle constantly, dealing with the presumption that he only hired me so we can be alone together, and

KELLEY ARMSTRONG

if we are alone together, it's clearly for sex. What else would he want with me?

If Lady Inglis has found a satisfying friendship-with-benefits relationship, I'm glad of it, for her sake. Although, given that it seems to have been going on for years, this might be the relationship that ended hers with Gray.

But I'm not thinking of that, so I'm not speculating on it. Nor am I glancing his way to gauge his reaction.

"You sent this friend letters of an intimate nature," I say. "And you are being blackmailed with them but not by him."

"They were stolen," she says. "He did not even realize they were missing until I received the threat. I contacted him immediately. He checked the locked box where he keeps them and found it empty."

"You received a threat. A letter?"

"Yes. I still have it, and I will show it to you after lunch. In short, the sender threatens to print my letters unless I pay. They included one letter as proof that they have them, which also told me who I'd written it for. I immediately checked with Lord—my friend, in case that was the only one missing, which would mitigate the threat. It was not."

"The blackmailer is threatening to print the letters...where?"

Another flush. "They are threatening to *publish* the letters. There is— That is to say, I have *heard* there is a taste for such things. The letters would be sold to a publisher of ill repute. That person would then print and sell them in a chapbook."

"I understand you would not want them published under any circumstances, but are the letters clearly identifiable as having been written by you?"

52

SCHEMES & SCANDALS

"No, but the blackmailer knows I am the writer—and that my friend is the recipient—and this person intends to reveal that."

I eat a few pieces of potato as I think. Then I say, "If we take the case, I will need to see the letter. Also, while I understand your desire for discretion, we will need to speak to your friend. Since he is also under threat—and he lost the letters in the first place—he will understand."

Lady Inglis sips from her wineglass. "Is that necessary?"

It's Gray who answers. "It is. As Miss Mitchell said, he lost the letters. They were taken from his home, I presume."

"Yes, but—"

"That makes this a theft, which we cannot investigate if we cannot see the scene and speak to the person who possessed the missing goods." He looks at her. "As I already know who we speak of, I do not see why you would shelter him." Gray pauses. "Unless he has asked to be sheltered."

"He has not," she says. "He is most distressed by this. I simply did not wish to involve him."

"He's already involved," I say. "He's also responsible. He chose to keep the letters, and his security was lacking. If you ask me, he's the one who should be paying the blackmailer."

"He has offered," Lady Inglis says. "I would not hear of it."

"Why not?"

She stares at me as if I've asked her to read the letters aloud. Yep, good thing I led with the warning about being blunt.

I continue, "This is entirely his fault. He should pay."

"I would agree," Gray says. "He chose to keep the letters and store them in an unsafe location, and yet the one who is truly under

KELLEY ARMSTRONG

threat is you. Yes, the blackmailer might say they will also reveal his name, but you are the one they expect to pay because you are the one who will suffer."

"They are still threatening him," Lady Inglis says.

"With what?" I say. "Telling the world that he's getting—"

Gray coughs, as if knowing whatever I was about to say was both improper and probably not a term currently in use.

"That he has a lover," I say. "A lover whom he inspires to write...er, letters of an erotic nature. That's not a threat. That's advertising."

Gray chokes on what might be a laugh. Lady Inglis stares, and then she lets loose a low chuckle.

"I take your meaning," she says. "I can assure you that my friend does not require advertising, but the point is that, as you said, I will suffer, and he will not. That is the way of the world."

"Yes, and highly unfair, but that's nothing we can rectify. So why not let him pay?"

She taps her fingers on the tablecloth, and it seems as if she isn't going to answer. Then she blurts, "Because it would put me in his debt." She pulls back, adding, "He is not the sort of person to use that to his advantage. We truly are friends. But in my experience, no matter how much a woman trusts a man, it is unwise to let him come to her rescue, particularly in matters of honor. If the blackmailer went to him, I would let him pay it. As I am the target, I wish to resolve this myself."

Okay, she's not as naive as she seemed with her earlier comments on honor. She has a point here. A good one.

"Can you pay?" I say.

SCHEMES & SCANDALS

She bristles. "I do not wish to."

"Let me rephrase that. I'm asking whether you could afford to and how easily."

She pauses and then says, "It is not what I consider pocket change, but it would hardly put me in the poorhouse. But even if it *were* pocket change, I do not wish to pay."

"I agree. You could pay this person and get the letters back, only to have them threaten you again with copies they have made. The only way to stop this is to uncover the blackmailer's identity." I take one last bite of potato. "How long do you have?"

"Only until Hogmanay. I received the demand a week ago, but I have been dithering, trying to determine what to do about it."

"May we see the blackmail letter now?" I ask.

"Certainly."

Six

LADY INGLIS brings us the letter over dessert. I note that it is coconut cake, one of Gray's favorites.

The letter has been pasted together from words in a newspaper. I'm impressed by that. I've only seen such things in movies, with ransom demands and the like, and it seems like a Hollywood invention, but I realize now it would date to a time before you could easily print off—or even type up—a letter.

We've had two cases now where handwriting played a role. If notes must be written by hand, even disguising penmanship is a tricky business. This person has been clever, cutting words from a newspaper.

```
Lady Inglis
    Enclosed you will find a letter of
yours that has come into my possession,
along with others. I will return them
```

KELLEY ARMSTRONG

for £500. I require the fee by Hogmanay, or I shall have them printed and sold. I do not think you or the recipient wish that.

On the morn of December 31, I will send along instructions for payment.

I read it again, and I must have grumbled under my breath because Gray says, "Something is wrong?"

I point at the last line. "This. The trickiest part about demanding a ransom is that you need to get the money somehow. You can specify a location to drop it off or a person to leave it with. Either provides a possible way to catch the blackmailer."

"Drop off the money and then wait to see who fetches it. If it is to be left with a person, question them."

"Because even if they've only been hired as an intermediary, *they* need to get the money to the blackmailer somehow."

Lady Inglis asks, "Is that the way to catch them, then? Wait for instructions?"

I shake my head. "Too risky, except as a last resort. They didn't leave much time between receiving instructions and following them. You'd need to pay and hope we catch the blackmailer." I cut off a mouthful-sized piece of my cake. "Instead of treating this as blackmail, we need to treat it as theft."

"Find out who stole the letters," Gray says.

"Yes. If we decide to take the case, I will need the name of your friend and his consent to be both interviewed and have the location of the theft examined."

SCHEMES & SCANDALS

"I will speak to him. I do not expect a problem. He is most distraught about this. Any reluctance to share his name is simply discretion, at least as much for my benefit as for his."

"I understand," I say. "If we take this case, you can be assured of *our* discretion. I'm not going to help a woman avoid exposure only to expose her myself. Before we agree to the case, Dr. Gray and I need to discuss the matter. We'll have an answer for you by this evening."

"Thank you. Now, we should discuss payment."

"Unnecessary," Gray says. "Consider it a favor between friends."

She fixes him with a steady look. "First, I believe I already clarified my feelings on owing men a debt for defending my honor. Second, as Miss Mitchell seems to be the one handling my case thus far, ought you to be turning down payment on her behalf?"

Gray had the grace to color at that. "Of course not. You may pay Miss Mitchell."

She turns to me. "I will do that. Your fee, miss?"

I resist the urge to demur. Taking wages from Gray still feels a bit like taking money from my host. I landed in his world—in the body of his housemaid—and he's stuck with me. Except I'm not a layabout guest, leeching off my hosts. I do my job, and I do it well. If Lady Inglis is offering to pay—and *wants* to pay—I should take her up on it. I also shouldn't insult either of us by undervaluing my services.

"Ten percent of the blackmail demand," I say. "If I identify the person responsible, I'll take ten percent. However, what you do with that information is up to you. I would suggest it goes to the police after that. Or, if it turns out to be someone you know, you can decide how to handle it."

"That is reasonable," Lady Inglis says. "Ten percent, then, for identifying the person behind this before I need to pay the ransom. You will decide whether to take this case and let me know by this evening."

"I will."

WE LEAVE AS soon as lunch is finished. I barely touched my cake. At home, that would have had Gray eyeing it, and I'd slide it over for him to finish. Even if I were in that sort of mood—which I am not—he doesn't even glance at my plate, and I notice his own cake is only half gone.

Lady Inglis accompanies us down the hall. Simon has the coach at the stable, and we'll walk to it rather than have a member of the staff run and fetch him. When we step out, Lady Inglis murmurs, "A word, please, Duncan?"

"I'll be at the stables," I say, not glancing to see his reaction.

"Wait," he says. "I will walk with you. The path can be uneven."

Uneven cobblestones are a fact of life in Victorian times, which makes it an odd excuse, but I don't argue. I pull my cloak tighter against the cold and step aside to wait as they talk.

"I really must be going," Gray says to Lady Inglis. "I do not want Miss Mitchell to take a tumble."

I shake my head. Really? That's the best he can come up with?

SCHEMES & SCANDALS

"This will only take a moment," Lady Inglis says.

Not wanting to eavesdrop, I walk around the corner of the house, only for Gray to call, "Mallory? Please do not wander."

Do not wander? Am I a sheep now?

I return to where Gray can see me, but unfortunately, I can still hear them, though I look the other way and pretend I can't.

"I wished to apologize," Lady Inglis says. "I was unspeakably churlish last night when I spoke of your relationship with Miss Mitchell."

"She is my assistant—"

"Yes. I see that now, which is why I am apologizing for insinuating anything else."

"I would not hire a young woman with the intention of being dishonorable."

She sighs. "I know, and I was wrong to suggest otherwise. I *do* know you better than that. Even if she were not your assistant, the mistake would have been an insult."

"An insult to…?" he says carefully.

She laughs softly. "To you, obviously, Duncan. While she is clearly intelligent, she is very young and…very much not to your taste. She is a peony. You prefer pansies."

Something in me bristles at that. Yes, Catriona has a very showy sort of beauty. There is nothing subtle or refined about it. But how she looks is a matter of genetics, and her personal style didn't take advantage of that any more than mine does. I'm dressed very primly, with more of my bosom hidden than is fashionable.

Gray's voice cools. "I would like to end this conversation now, Patricia."

KELLEY ARMSTRONG

"I'm not insulting Miss Mitchell, Duncan. She is a spectacularly lovely girl, with a keen intelligence. Were she a decade older, I would be jealous."

"Which you have no reason to be, as you and I are no longer together."

Another deep sigh. "That is not what I meant. I know you are no longer interested in me, and I respect that. I only mean that I would find myself envying any woman who caught your eye. It reminds me that I caught it once upon a time, and I was careless, which I regret very much."

"I do not see the point of this conversation," Gray says. "I would suggest we end it."

"I never say the right thing to you, do I?" she murmurs, and there's something in her voice that makes me feel sorry for Lady Inglis. What happened to end her relationship with Gray wasn't her fault—he hadn't made it clear he expected monogamy. It was a misunderstanding that led to hurt pride, which cost her someone she obviously cared for.

"It is fine," Gray murmurs, and his tone is conciliatory, but he adds a firm, "I really must be going. I will send you a message this evening with our decision."

Seven

WE'RE IN the coach. Gray hasn't said a word since he caught up with me, and now he's staring silently out the window as we pull away.

I clear my throat. "I'm going to take the case. You are free to stay out of it, as I'm not really a hapless twenty-year-old in need of guidance."

"No," he says, looking back at me sharply. "I said if you did this, I would, too, and—"

"And I'm sick of circling, so let's skip this shit, okay?"

The profanity startles him out of an answer.

I continue, "Working with Lady Inglis makes you uncomfortable, and it's not necessary. That's my point, Duncan. You don't need to do this. I can handle it on my own."

His tone chills. "If you do not wish my assistance, say so."

I slam back in my seat with a profanity that has him blinking.

"I give up," I say. "You're upset about this whole thing, and you're taking it out on me. I'm doing backflips to accommodate you, and you're determined to see insult in anything I say." I meet

KELLEY ARMSTRONG

his gaze. "You're right, Duncan. I don't want your assistance. Because you're being an ass, and I did nothing to deserve it."

"I—"

"You insisted on accepting Lady Inglis's offer to introduce me to Mr. Dickens, knowing it could put you in her debt. I'm accepting that debt as the person who benefited from it. But I still wouldn't feel obligated to take the case. I'm choosing to do so because no woman deserves what this person is doing to her. She's an unattached woman engaging in consensual affairs and having some fun writing risqué letters to her partners. This person is threatening to brand her with a scarlet letter, and that's wrong."

When he says nothing, I add, "Scarlet letter means—"

"Yes, I have read the book. I understand the reference. You are correct, of course. Lady Inglis's affairs are no one's business but her own, as are any letters she might write."

He leans back in his seat. "You are also correct that I am uncomfortable with the situation and taking it out on you, which I am wont to do."

"Yep."

He gives me a sidelong glance.

"Oh, I'm sorry," I say. "Am I supposed to say that you *don't* do that? Or that you hardly *ever* do it?"

He doesn't answer, but I know that I *am* supposed to do that. He is a Victorian male, head of the household in which I reside, and if he deigns to admit to a failing, I should fall over myself to reassure him it's fine. Okay, maybe "fall over myself" is an exaggeration, but even someone as progressive as Gray has certain expectations. Or certain hopes, at least, because there is not a

68

SCHEMES & SCANDALS

woman in his household who'd tell him he's fine when he's screwing up. Except maybe Mrs. Wallace.

Gray sighs, and it is such a deeply chagrined sigh that I have to fight against falling for it. I should be annoyed that he expects reassurances—or at least praise—when he admits to a failing, but he's a man of his time, and I find it oddly charming. Of course, it's charming because I know he genuinely tries to do better.

Growing up, I hated it when people told me I was lucky to have loving parents who supported me and my choices. How was it "lucky" to have parents who did what decent parents should do? Yet I do consider myself lucky to have landed in Gray's household, where even before he knew I wasn't Catriona, he'd been happy to take me on as his assistant. What mattered was that I was capable, regardless of my sex. That's how it should be, of course, but how a thing should be is not the same as how it is.

I'd had a much greater chance of landing in a house where I'd be stuck cleaning chamber pots and fending off my boss's wandering hands, because that's what happened to girls like Catriona.

I *am* lucky that Gray is as forward-thinking as he is. I *am* fortunate that he accepts criticism from me. But I can still roll my eyes when he expects a cookie for admitting to a failing. These things are not incompatible.

"May I join your investigation, Miss Mitchell?" he says.

I straighten. "Oooh, I like the sounds of that. Polite and contrite. Say it again."

He only sighs.

"Fine," I say. "You may join it on the understanding that if you get pissy again, I can kick you out."

KELLEY ARMSTRONG

"Even if I get 'pissy' over something you do?"

"Impossible. I am perfection personified."

Now I get the eye roll. Deservedly.

"Also, you're joining in a volunteer capacity," I say. "All the money is mine."

He sobers. "As it should be. However, if you are taking the case for the money, I can always increase—"

"I said I'm taking the case on principle. I'm just letting her pay because she can afford it. My salary is more than sufficient. So we'll drop that." I rearrange my skirts as the December chill creeps up from the carriage floor. "On an equally serious note, though, the reason I didn't take the job right away is that I do want to discuss it with you."

"All right."

"And if discussing it with you touches on any personal matters that make you uncomfortable, you need to acknowledge that I'm asking for the case. I'm not trying to make you uncomfortable or pry into your personal life."

He shifts, and I inwardly sigh. This is exactly what I'm afraid of. That every time the case brushes up against his past with Lady Inglis, there's going to be resistance and friction.

"This first question is actually not about the case directly, but I have to bring it up." I clear my throat. "I know Lady Inglis sent you a letter after you ended things. Did she send others before that?"

"No. We did not… That is to say…" He plucks at his collar. "If this is a habit of hers, she must have decided I was not the properly receptive audience for it."

SCHEMES & SCANDALS

"Or, more likely, she only does it with this one longtime friend. The reason I'm asking is to be sure you're not at risk yourself."

"I am not. Any other correspondence I received was not of that nature, and I destroyed it shortly after receipt. I realize that may seem cold, not keeping such letters for sentimental reasons, but I do it out of an abundance of caution. As you said at lunch, I would not be faulted for such entanglements, but the women would be. Destroying their letters seems wise."

"Agreed," I say. "And I was going to say that if she did send you any more intimate ones, you should destroy them."

He glances at me. "The one she did send, you burned, yes?"

"I did." I adjust the muff keeping my hands warm. "You said you think you know the man involved. The one whose letters were stolen."

I expect his tone to chill—or at least his gaze to—but he only nods. "I am certain I know him. They have been longtime friends, as Lady Inglis said, and I knew they'd been lovers. Because you will likely not ask, yes, he is the one I discovered she'd been seeing while we were together."

"Is that going to be a problem?" I hear myself and rephrase. "I'm sure that'll make the interview uncomfortable. I can conduct that part."

"Hmm?" He looks genuinely surprised. "No, it isn't... That is to say, it's not like that. I have no issue with Lord— With the person involved. The mistake was honestly mine. I knew they had been involved, and I did not necessarily think the affair had ended, but he was living abroad while I was seeing Lady Inglis.

KELLEY ARMSTRONG

When he returned, I heard that she had gone to see him. I did not want to presume anything, so I asked and..."

He gives a rueful smile. "I discovered that their relationship was ongoing. That was it. I did not walk in on them together. Even her visit to his house was purely platonic, a luncheon with others. But she made it clear that he was still intimately part of her life, and I took it poorly and left. No dramatic encounter. Merely a misunderstanding."

"Still upsetting."

He looks out the window a moment before turning to me. "And still a misunderstanding for which no one else is to blame. If I do blame him for anything, it is only *this* unfortunate incident with the letter. Even then, I doubt that he was careless with them. It is understandable to keep them, and he seems to have locked them away."

"How well do you know him?"

"Not terribly well," Gray says. "I did meet Lady Inglis through him, though. We attend the same club, and he has an interest in medical science and asked me to accompany him to the surgical theater. We did that a few times, and I met Lady Inglis at a party he hosted before he went to Europe on an extended trip. I have seen him since, at the club, and we have been cordial."

"Cordial but cool?"

The corners of Gray's mouth twitch upward. "I am always cool, Mallory. It is my natural demeanor. If you are asking whether I was cooler because of the misunderstanding, I do not think so. I am not even certain he knew I was seeing Lady Inglis in his absence."

I tap my fingers inside my muff as I think. "Whoever stole the letters had access to this man's home."

"Yes."

SCHEMES & SCANDALS

"What kind of home does he keep? He's a lord, which might mean he has multiple residences."

"As I understand it, he has only one. A town house perhaps a mile from ours, where he lives with his younger brother. As for Lord…" He trails off.

"Joe," I say. "Until Lady Inglis releases his name, let's go with Lord Joe."

Another twitch of the lips. "All right. Lord Joe is a widower himself. Only a few years older than Lady Inglis. He lost his wife a year before Lady Inglis lost her husband."

"And the younger brother?"

Gray's expression at that has me leaning forward.

"You do not like the brother?"

"I do not know him well, but he does attend our club, and he is a sanctimonious— I find him unpleasant. Lord Joe is very convivial, but he clearly inherited all the charm in the family."

"Lord Joe is convivial. Can I assume that means he entertains regularly? Has a steady stream of guests who could have stolen the letters?"

"He has a great many friends. He does not entertain in the usual way, having no lady of the house to organize such events, but he would have guests. Yes, I fear, the list of suspects might not be as small as we hope."

"But it's still a constrained number. Whoever stole the letters had access to the house."

"Yes."

Eight

I USHER JACK into the library, where Isla waits. Jack is our new housemaid. She's also the writer of our chronicles, as part of her double life as an anonymous chronicler of Edinburgh crime. Double life? Make that triple life or even quadruple. Jack has endless irons in the fire, and when she says her chosen moniker comes from "Jack of all trades," I'm not sure she's joking, but I always follow up with "master of none," because she's just asking for that one.

The choice of a masculine moniker isn't accidental, either. In public, she usually wears male attire. I wouldn't call it a disguise as much as a choice. She goes by female pronouns and keeps her hair long enough that she needs to put it up in a cap for the male persona. In our world, she'd be considered gender fluid.

During work hours at the town house, Jack wears a dress. Isla has made it clear that isn't necessary, and certainly, *I'd* have much rather cleaned in trousers. Easier to move in and *much* easier to bend in. I think Jack makes the choice to present as a female maid because it's easier for Gray and Isla, saving them from adding to

KELLEY ARMSTRONG

the heap of eccentricities that already puts them on the fringe of their social class. If I'd told Isla I wanted to clean in trousers, she'd have let me. I didn't for this exact reason.

Jack's work dress is like my old one, simple and blue. Victorian households haven't yet adopted uniforms, but Isla provides work clothing so her employees don't need to buy it themselves, and she sticks to a blue-and-white color scheme and well-made attire.

Before Isla hired Jack—or, more accurately, accepted Jack's work proposal—I'd only ever seen Jack present as male, so I'm still getting used to her feminine persona. As male, she looks in her late teens, very slender and fine featured. As a woman, she's obviously in her early twenties, with gorgeous red-brown hair that answers the question of why she doesn't cut it to better suit her male persona.

I wave Jack to a chair and shut the door.

"I have called you both here today to discuss something of great import." I look from one to the other. "Pornography."

Isla stares at me.

Jack bursts into snickers and says, "Please tell me you actually meant to say 'pornography,' Mallory, and you haven't simply misused a word again."

Jack doesn't know my real identity. She's been given the cover story—that a blow to Catriona's head changed her personality and she now goes by Mallory. Also, the blow affected Catriona's memory, and she sometimes gets confused, especially with vocabulary, misusing words or making up new ones altogether.

"Yes, I meant 'pornography.' We have a case that involves it, and I need opinions."

"On…pornography?" Jack says.

SCHEMES & SCANDALS

"Mallory is having fun with us," Isla says. "This is not the first time she's managed to connect a case to illicit material of a pornographic nature."

"Managed to connect?" I say. "The connection was there. We had a suspect who moonlighted as a nude model."

"Moonlighted?" Jack says.

"Whatever the word is. She worked a secret job. This is different. We now have a case where a woman…" I curse under my breath as I see Jack lean forward. I forgot how *she* moonlights.

"A case?" Jack says, eyes gleaming.

"Not a case for public consumption. Certainly not for your chronicles of our cases. It is a woman being threatened with exposure for writings…of an erotic nature."

Jack's brows climb.

I continue, "She wrote it for an audience of one, but the work has been stolen, and she is being blackmailed by the thief."

"Sadly, I could not use this in our chronicles," Jack says. She quickly adds, "Not that I would. It'd be wrong. But even if I could, it is not the sort of case your audience wants."

"Our audience being women who can read murder mysteries to their children under the guise of providing didactic tales to prove that no crime goes unpunished."

Isla sniffs. "In this case, the crime *some* would see is that a woman dared pen such things and was, in their minds, rightfully threatened with punishment."

"Either way," Jack says, "it would be inappropriate. Depictions of gruesome murder, yes. The mention of writings exploring sexuality?" She shudders. "Think of the children."

KELLEY ARMSTRONG

I want to roll my eyes at the very Victorian-ness of this. And then I remember the childhood friend who was allowed to rent any action or horror movie, however violent, as long as it didn't contain nudity.

I can still blame the Victorians, right? They started it.

Okay, it was probably the Puritans, who passed it on to the Victorians, but still...

Isla says, "I presume the blackmailer is threatening to expose this poor woman as a pornographer?"

"Worse," I say. "They're threatening to *make* her a pornographer. To have her writings published and sold, with her name attached."

"Published and sold?" Isla's brows knit. "Is that profitable?"

Both Jack and I turn to stare at her.

"Is pornography profitable?" Jack says slowly. "If that is your question, Mrs. Ballantyne, I fear you are more sheltered than I thought."

Isla glares at both of us. "I know pornographic sketches and photography are profitable. I mean this sort. Writing that is purely intimate in nature, rather than part of a larger narrative, such as *Fanny Hill*."

"You've read *Fanny Hill*, Mrs. Ballantyne?" Jack says.

Isla's glare locks on her. "I read everything, and if you expect me to sputter and flush, I will not."

"Actually," I say, "your question is the reason I called you both in here. I don't know whether things like this are popular or easily sold. I could ask Dr. Gray, but he really *would* sputter, as well as turn a very unhealthy shade of red and, ultimately, not answer the question."

SCHEMES & SCANDALS

"But you thought *I* could?" Isla says.

"Hey, you just said you read everything."

"Having not known this sort of writing existed, I have not read it."

I grin at her. "Good. Then I know what to get you for Hogmanay."

She does sputter and flush at that, then skewers me with a glare that says I will pay for this.

I turn to Jack. "How about you? As a writer, would you say there's a market for letters like this?"

Jack stretches her legs and then remembers she's wearing a skirt and retracts them. "There is certainly an audience for such work. Putting it into a larger narrative—particularly if one can pass it off as proper literature—is one way to do it, but there is a very avid market for those who do not want story interfering with the risqué bits. It can pay exceedingly well. I tried it myself but…" She shrugs. "I am better at writing about murder. That problem, to be honest, seems to be a lack of experience."

"You have more experience with murder than sex?" I say.

She sighs. "I strode into that one, didn't I? No, it's not even a lack of experience with sexual congress so much as a lack of experience with *good* sexual congress. No one wants to read about the bad stuff, even if it's embellished by imagination."

"I feel I should offer my condolences," I say. "I would also suggest you stop bothering with the bad stuff."

"And how would you suggest I do that? Ask men whether they're any good first? They all think they're incredible because *they* finish every time. This is one place where I truly envy men."

"For being able to finish every time?"

KELLEY ARMSTRONG

"Well, yes, but beyond that, men can easily obtain good sex by paying for it. Go to a brothel and lay down money for a woman of craft and experience. Women do not have that option. We have to take what we can get and hope for the best, which is *never* the best, no matter what the men claim."

I glance at Isla, who is sitting perfectly still, with the expression of a twelve-year-old hearing teen girls talk about sex, trying to look casual, as if she hears this all the time, as if she's not inwardly shocked that they're openly discussing *it* the way one discusses the weather.

As I've said, women in this time do discuss sex, but only among themselves and, from what I can tell, primarily among the lower classes. Jack would have no problem with it, and she'd presume I wouldn't, either.

I also note that Isla doesn't stop us or even give us a scandalized look. Like that preteen girl, she's soaking it up.

"So there is an audience for this," I say, bringing the conversation back around. "How profitable would it be?"

"How much is the blackmail for?" Jack asks.

"Five hundred pounds."

Jack whistles. "It would *never* be that profitable. The primary audience for such writing, from a woman's perspective, would likely be women themselves. In written work, that audience is larger."

"Men prefer pictures?"

She laughs softly. "They do. Women prefer narrative where they may fill in their own imagination. Probably because they have so much experience doing that while lying under a heaving, grunting, sweaty man."

SCHEMES & SCANDALS

"You really need to cultivate a better class of partners," I say.

She sighs. "I know. But while the audience for such things is largely women, it still is smaller than the audience for visual pornography, and even that would not come close to the price the blackmailer is demanding."

"Meaning they really are counting on our client paying the ransom."

"Yes. The blackmailer is not necessarily bluffing about publishing them. Such things could be sold for a nice bit of income. But that also requires knowing *where* to sell it, which the average person would not."

"But you do?"

"I do, and if it comes to that, we could attempt to avoid publication by paying the printer for the return of the materials. But that would not be easily done."

"So we should presume the threat is serious and try to find the blackmailer before those letters reach a printer."

"I fear so."

Nine

GRAY HAS told Lady Inglis that we're taking her case. By morning, we have an invitation from "Lord Charles Simpson" to join him at his home. We accept, and at ten, Simon drops us outside Lord Simpson's town house.

The town house is similar to Gray's. Maybe a bit smaller. We're entering an era where it's not uncommon for the middle class to have more money than the nobility. It's the rise of the industrial era, where investing in a trade can earn you more than having a title and a bit of land.

Simpson certainly still lives very well. Cross into the Old Town, and his place would house multiple families on each of its four levels. My impression is that he is averagely well-to-do for a viscount, which is what I expected.

Lord Simpson himself, however, is not what I expected. I've met Lady Inglis—beautiful, cultured, and wealthy. Her lover will be her male equivalent. I know he's a few years older than her, so I picture a dashing and distinguished silver fox. A bon vivant who can capture and hold a woman like Lady Inglis.

KELLEY ARMSTRONG

When the butler leads us into the parlor, I see a man and remember that Lord Simpson lives with his younger brother. I presume that's who I'm seeing. The man is rotund, with jet-black hair and equally dark whiskers. When he turns, I see he's older than I thought, and the very dark hair likely comes from a bottle.

"Lord Charles Simpson," the butler says. "May I present Dr. Duncan Gray and Miss Mallory Mitchell."

Okay, this was not what I expected, but that's on me, isn't it? Lady Inglis is an intelligent and discerning woman who will expect more than a handsome face in her lovers, and the sparkle in Simpson's eye suggests the bon vivant I imagined.

"Dr. Gray," he says, taking Gray's hand. "It has been too long. So good to see you. And Miss Mitchell. Welcome. I am so pleased to hear that Dr. Gray has found a proper assistant. The last time we spoke, he was having a terrible time with that."

Simpson engages in a few moments of small talk, striking the perfect balance between being a convivial host and recognizing that we're here on business. When he asks after our health, it's in that way some people have of making you feel they actually care about the answer. Then it's a quick exchange on the weather and how the cold is a nuisance but the snow is lovely, and there seems to be actual sunshine today, yes?

By the time that's done, a maid arrives with a tea tray. He tells her to shut the door behind her and warns that this is business and he'd rather not be disturbed unless it is urgent. Once she's gone, he pours the tea before speaking.

"You are investigating the missing letters," he says.

SCHEMES & SCANDALS

"We are," Gray says. "Lady Inglis requested my help, and while it is not my area of expertise…"

"I have heard you are doing some detective work," Simpson says. "With the police. Consulting on murders and such. You really must let me take you out to dinner, Gray, so I may ask all about that. I am *fascinated*. The idea of using science to solve murders? Brilliant. Can you imagine where such a thing could lead? In a hundred years, if a person is murdered, science could lead us straight to the killer and prove they did it. No need for police to investigate nor for lawyers and judges to try the case. Science will prove guilt beyond a shadow of a doubt."

Gray sneaks a look at me, but I see no point in poking a hole in Simpson's enthusiasm. It's like telling modern people that the idea of flying cars doesn't actually, well, fly. Let them dream.

"That would be lovely, wouldn't it?" I say. "As for this case, we're focusing on it as a theft. Finding who stole the letters will lead us to the blackmailer."

"Miss Mallory will ask most of the questions," Gray says. "This is far more her area than mine."

"An excellent partnership, then," Simpson says. "Before we begin, while it has no bearing on the case, you must forgive me for needing to get it off my chest."

He sets his cup into the saucer. "I am horrified by what has happened. It is entirely my fault. I thought I had properly secured Patricia's letters, and clearly, I had not. I desperately wish that this scoundrel had sent the demand to me instead. I would have paid it with Patricia being none the wiser."

"It went to her because her reputation is the one at risk," I say.

KELLEY ARMSTRONG

"I know," he says mournfully. "She is in danger because of my mistake. I only wish she would allow me to pay this scoundrel."

"She prefers not to pay at all," I say. "If you wish to make it up to her, then the best way to do that is to help us find the blackmailer."

"Certainly. You have my full cooperation." He pulls a piece of paper from his pocket. "I have recorded all the details here. I kept the letters in my room, in a locked box on my dressing table. I know that it was locked December twentieth, as I also keep some jewelry in there and opened it to retrieve that for a seasonal gala. I returned the items that night and relocked it. I did not realize it was unlocked until Patricia notified me of the theft." He checks his notes. "On the morning of December twenty-third."

"You didn't notice the box had been opened?" I ask.

"The lock is not an obvious one. I will show it to you. It is impossible to tell at a glance whether it is locked or not."

"You said it's kept in your bedroom. Is that door locked?"

He looks confused by the question. I don't blame him. In a world of household staff, a bedroom door is rarely locked. Maids and valets need access to it.

"No," he says. "There is a lock, but I rarely use it."

"So everyone on your staff has access."

He shifts in obvious discomfort. "Yes. I…" He coughs. "I am about to say something that distresses me. I am very aware of how quick people are to blame the servants for anything that goes missing, and normally, that infuriates me."

"But…" I prod.

"I dismissed my valet on the twenty-first. I am planning another trip abroad in the new year, and he…is not properly suited

82

SCHEMES & SCANDALS

to continental travel. I told him I was happy to keep him on until I left, but he said he would rather spend the holidays with family. I gave him a quarter's wages, and it all seemed very amicable, but then Patricia received this demand two days later..."

"Do you know where we might find this valet?"

Another shift of discomfort. "I do, but might I ask that you do not say I sent you?"

"We will say that we required a list of all staff employed at the time of the theft, and that you assured us none of your staff would have done this, but we insisted."

He exhales. "Thank you. I have spoken to all of my staff. I said that private correspondence had disappeared and asked if any of them might have seen it. I was hoping that if one did take the letters, they would quietly return them, and we could be done with the matter. That did not happen."

"You also have a brother, I understand, who lives with you."

Simpson blinks. "Arthur? Of course, but he would not have done this."

"We'll need to speak to him. I'll also need a list of every guest who was in the house between the twentieth and the twenty-third."

"No one," he says. "I went out a fair deal, but Arthur and I did not entertain."

"So no one came to the house? No friends? No business associates?"

"It is not the time of year for business. Lady Inglis visited on the twenty-first, but that was it."

"No one else?" I meet his gaze, my look silently reminding him of his promise to cooperate.

"No one," he says firmly. "You may ask the staff. I had a guest on the nineteenth, but that was before the theft. I hosted a small luncheon on the twenty-fifth, but that was after the letters were taken."

"Your guest on the nineteenth..."

"Could not have stolen the letters," he says. "They were there when I opened the box the evening of the twentieth, and she had been gone since that morning."

She. A woman who spent the night. A lover who is not Lady Inglis. That would be a promising lead, except that the timing doesn't work.

"Might I see the box and where it is kept?" I ask.

"Certainly."

AS SIMPSON SAID, the box is on his dresser, in plain sight. I inwardly sigh at that. It's a pretty box, inlaid with mother-of-pearl, and it screams "I contain valuables!" It's about six inches by four inches, meaning it could easily be stolen whole and broken open for the contents.

The lock makes me sigh again. It's the sort Victorians are terribly fond of. A puzzle lock. Yet the puzzle is so simple that I get it after a few minutes, to Simpson's astonishment. It seems clever enough, but if you've played with puzzle locks, you'd recognize this one.

I like Simpson. He seems like a lovely man. But he really needs to work on his plan for safeguarding private letters. In his defense,

SCHEMES & SCANDALS

he strikes me as the trusting sort, a fellow who'd make the mistake of presuming that if a box clearly contains something private, his staff and guests would respect that.

Anyone who had access to this room could have stolen the letters. And anyone with access to the house had access to the room.

"May I take the box?" I ask. "For closer inspection?"

Gray frowns my way. Then he understands. I want to dust it for fingerprints. I'm not sure that will do any good, but it's worth a shot. Simpson agrees, and I ask a few more questions. Then we take our leave.

Gray and I head down the street, a light snow falling around us.

"The valet and the brother," I say. "Those are my primary suspects. We have the valet's information, but the brother is trickier. I get the sense that, as cooperative as Lord Simpson wants to be, he'd rather we didn't question his brother."

"Because the man is an insufferable prig," Gray says. He makes a face. "That was rude of me."

"But true?"

"Arthur Simpson is the sort of younger son one expects to join the clergy. He is insufferably sanctimonious and makes it clear that he finds his brother's lifestyle decadently sinful. However, there's a reason Arthur never joined the clergy—he has a dear love of decadence himself. His simply doesn't extend to what *he* considers sinful."

"Taking lovers."

"Yes, though at the risk of seeming a terrible person, I might suggest that jealousy rather than piety fuels his outrage."

"Ah, he's not half as charming as his brother."

KELLEY ARMSTRONG

"Not a *tenth* as charming. I can understand why Lord Simpson wouldn't want Arthur knowing about the missing letters, but I agree he's an excellent suspect. Even better than a fired valet. I also think I know a way we might encounter Arthur, quite by accident, of course."

I smile. "Perfect."

Ten

IT TURNS out that "perfect" is not quite the word I should have used. The place where we can find the younger Simpson brother? His club, which I may not enter because I am a woman.

I don't think I realized exactly how many Victorian venues were off-limits to middle- and upper-class ladies. There are men's clubs, which I would have guessed. Also, brothels and gambling halls and fight clubs. Gymnasiums, too, so that men might exercise in peace. And pubs, so they might drink in peace. That mostly applies to upper-class pubs, but in that sphere, the restriction carries over to all dining establishments where liquor might be served. Men must be free to drink and conduct business without women around.

I can be shocked by the number of places a woman like Isla can't go, but within my own lifetime, there have been countless modern venues where women were barred, either outright or by practice. Places where men went to relax and drink and socialize and talk business.

KELLEY ARMSTRONG

Gray will need to conduct this interview alone. I'm fine with that. Okay, "fine" might be an exaggeration, but I accept it…as long as he grants me permission to try sneaking in and eavesdropping. I really do need to ask permission for that. Gray might not require the women in his household to seek it, but patriarchies work both ways. If I'm caught, he'll be the one punished for not properly "controlling" me.

He agrees to me sneaking in and provides some tips for where I might be able to enter. In return, I promise that if it seems risky, I'll back out.

I get inside the club easily enough. It's not as if they guard the entrance against women. It *is* guarded, but with an elderly man whose real job is making sure no male riffraff sneak through. Members and their guests only.

I slip in through a side door, where I only catch the curious glance of someone's coach driver resting in a tiny room that seems to be for that purpose. With men staying in the club for hours— and no easy way to resummon their driver—that little room is a necessity. Or, I guess, not a necessity so much as a perk. Otherwise, they'd be expected to hang out in the stable.

The driver only tips his hat to me, presuming I'm staff coming in for a shift. Women *are* allowed in places like this. Just not as members or guests.

From there, it gets trickier because if I meet an actual staff member, they'll know I don't belong. It takes me twenty minutes to get near the main rooms—I have to keep backtracking and ducking to avoid notice. Eventually, I find what I'm looking for, and can I just say that for an upscale gentlemen's club, it's sorely

SCHEMES & SCANDALS

disappointing. It looks like a fancy airport lounge. A few big rooms with chairs and fireplaces...and that's about it. The chairs are arranged in pods for conversation, and there's a low murmur of that, but at least half the men are alone, reading newspapers or books with a cup of tea at their elbow.

I've approached through a back hall, where I can sneak peeks through discreet viewing ports, and I'm not sure whether that makes me feel like a voyeur or a visitor to the zoo.

Here you see the upper-crust Victorian male in his natural habitat, smoking a pipe and reading the newspaper, doing things he could also do at home, but then he might need to... I don't know, talk to his wife? Acknowledge his children?

I presume the viewing ports are so the staff can be ready to refill those teacups or empty those ashtrays as efficiently as possible.

When I hear Gray's voice, I follow it down another corridor. I peek out and see him sitting with a man who, again, surprises me. He's clearly Simpson's brother, given the resemblance, but Arthur looks more like the lover I pictured for Lady Inglis, handsome and polished. As I said, looks aren't everything, and it doesn't take long to understand why Lady Inglis would prefer the elder Simpson.

"Don't beat about the bush, Gray," Arthur snaps. "I am not a fool. I know what happens in my own home. Charles keeps a secret as well as a boy in short pants. Someone has stolen private letters from his room. Letters that ought to have been burned the moment he realized what they were. Ladies these days are not what they used to be. They are not *ladies* at all."

"Yes, your brother is missing letters of an intimate nature—"

KELLEY ARMSTRONG

"Intimate? Pornographic, that is what they are."

Gray pauses, and I try to see him, but the angle is wrong, and I doubt I'd see anything but a studiously blank expression.

"You have read them?" Gray says mildly.

That gets a satisfying spate of apoplectic sputtering from Arthur Simpson.

Gray says, "You seem to know what the letters contain—"

"Because he accidentally left one lying about and I picked it up, innocently thinking it a simple bit of correspondence, only to read…" He sputters some more. "Filth one should never find outside a brothel. And the most deviant of brothels at that."

Read the whole thing, didn't you, Arthur?

"Do they have such letters in brothels?" Gray says, his tone still so delightfully mild. "Are they intended for reading while you wait for one of the ladies to be available?"

More sputtering as Arthur insists he has no idea what is in brothels, and he was merely making a point.

Gray lets him go on a bit before interrupting. "So you are aware of the missing letters."

"Yes, I am aware. I could hardly miss Charles rushing about the house, whispering to all the servants, asking whether they had seen any 'letters' from a box he keeps locked on his dresser. I waited for him to come to me. He did not, because he knows I would never knowingly soil my mind with such things."

"Do you have any idea who might have taken them?"

"No, but if it finally forces my brother to make an honest woman of that tart, then I shall owe them my gratitude."

"That tart being…"

SCHEMES & SCANDALS

Disgust oozes from Arthur's voice. "You know who wrote the letters as well as I do, Gray. Lady Inglis. My brother's mistress. One of them, at least."

"You do not seem fond of Lady Inglis, though you wish her for a sister-in-law?"

"I am not fond of any of his tarts, but at least *she* is respectable. Outwardly respectable, that is. A widow from a fine family. Still attractive. Clever enough. Well-liked and—" He seems to need to force himself to say the words. "—well-mannered. Charles would do well to marry her and stop this…behavior. I do not know why she puts up with him, but she obviously does and has for years. He is not a young man anymore, and he should not act like one. It is an embarrassment."

"You think the letters will lead to a marriage proposal?"

"Of course. Whoever has stolen them obviously intends to blackmail Charles. He cannot afford to pay a ransom, so he will be forced to marry her. Finally."

I peek out to see Arthur sipping his tea while Gray steeples his fingers, as if in quiet thought.

After a moment, Arthur says, "I would not be surprised if she stole the letters herself."

"Lady Inglis?"

"Certainly." Arthur leans forward, his tone almost excited, as if he has just solved the mystery. "Now that this new girl has entered the picture, Lady Inglis realizes she is never going to have him to herself without a wedding ring. She steals the letters—easily done, as she has access to my brother's bedchamber. Then she threatens him with a ransom he cannot pay, and he

KELLEY ARMSTRONG

has no choice but to marry her before this thief takes their affair public."

Arthur lowers his voice and says, "Cleverly done, ma'am. Cleverly done indeed." He rubs his hands together. "There. This is settled. He shall need to marry the woman and be done with it."

"I am surprised you are so eager to see Charles wed," Gray murmurs. "After all, as his first marriage was childless, his title would pass to you and your sons, should you have any. If he marries Lady Inglis, he might still have a son."

Arthur laughs. "She is nearly forty, and she did not bear her first husband any heirs. I am hardly worried..." He trails off and then says, "I wish to see my brother wed. That is all. If he is fond of Lady Inglis, I see no reason for this mistress nonsense."

"You mentioned a new girl—"

Someone clears their throat right beside me, making me stagger back and miss the rest of what Gray says. A severe-looking woman in a dour brown dress stands there with her arms crossed.

"May I help you, miss?" she says.

"Oh!" I clap my hands to my mouth. "Oh!"

"Do not tell me you are one of the serving girls," she says. "As I am in *charge* of the serving girls, I know you are not."

"N-no," I fake-stammer. "I am not. I am... I am so sorry, ma'am." I give an awkward half curtsy. "I... know I should not be here, but I followed that gentleman in." I wave toward the viewing port. "The older one, with the light-brown hair," I say, describing Arthur Simpson.

Her face darkens. "You followed one of our members into his private club?"

92

SCHEMES & SCANDALS

"I am so sorry, ma'am. I am ashamed of myself and truly appalled by my boldness, but it comes from desperation. I hoped I might hear someone address him by his name."

"His name?" The woman looks through the hole and then glowers at me. "If you are looking for a wealthy gentleman to keep you in comfort—"

"No!" I round my eyes in shock. "No, ma'am. I am a respectable young woman. I am a shop clerk, over on Princes Street. I would never be a kept woman. It is only that…that I made that gentleman's acquaintance, from my shop, and I…" I bite my lip. "I found him handsome and let him take me rowing, and now I most desperately need to speak to him about…" I let my hands slide to my stomach before pulling them away. "A private matter."

"You do not even know his name?"

I drop my gaze. "He gave me one, ma'am, but I have learned it is false."

She glowers again, but this time, it's aimed at the viewing port. "His name is Arthur Simpson." She turns that hard look my way. "But you did not hear it from me."

I bow and scrape and stammer my thanks, and then I let her lead me to the nearest door.

I MEET GRAY outside the club about twenty minutes later. I don't tell him I got caught, and I certainly don't tell him how I got out of it. He might not like Arthur Simpson, but he'd still feel guilty knowing that one of the club's staff wrongly thinks Arthur

KELLEY ARMSTRONG

knocked up a shop girl. He'd be wrong, of course. By the end of the day, *all* the club's staff will think that, and I personally don't feel the least bit guilty.

"You managed to get inside, then?" Gray says.

"I did, and I was sorely disappointed by the lack of dancing girls."

He stops midstride. "Dancing girls?"

"Dancing girls, maybe a few dancing boys… What kind of gentlemen's club is that?"

He gives me a sidelong look as he resumes walking. "So in your world, a gentlemen's club has…dancing girls?"

"Strippers."

"And strippers are dancers who…?"

"Pretty sure it's right there in the name, Gray."

He turns the most adorable shade of mahogany.

I continue. "To be honest, though, while they call themselves gentlemen's clubs, it's not quite the same thing. In my world, that's just a fancy name for a place where you can watch naked women sliding on poles."

He chokes so violently that his eyes water.

"Not sliding on them like that," I say. "Get your mind out of the gutter. If you want that, you need to go to Amsterdam."

"Amster…"

"It's a city in—"

"I have visited Amsterdam."

"And you missed the sex shows? What kind of tourist are you?" I continue walking. "As for your club, it was boring. I didn't honestly expect dancing girls, but there wasn't even a heated game of

94

SCHEMES & SCANDALS

chess. Now I know why you don't let women in. So they don't see how dull you all are. *Ah, yes, let us go to our secret club and drink tea and smoke cigars.* How scandalous!"

He only shakes his head. "As for the case…"

"Fine," I say with a deep sigh. "Drag me back on point."

"Yes, I am as dull as my gentlemen's club."

I could go along with it and tease him. But I find myself leaning to tap my winter bonnet against his shoulder and murmuring, "You are never dull, Duncan."

"I know."

I have to laugh. "Do you?"

"Of course. If I were dull, you would not stand my company for one moment longer than necessary. Did you hear my questioning of the younger Simpson?"

"Enough to think him a very fine suspect. I love it when my suspects are assholes. Makes my job a true delight." I glance over, catching his expression. "You disagree?"

"About preferring heinous suspects? Not at all. But while I think Arthur is eager to see his brother wed to Lady Inglis—especially as she is unlikely to provide an heir—stealing the letters will not do that. Lord Simpson likes his current lifestyle. Note that he was quick to offer to pay the ransom but not to marry her. He won't."

"But does Arthur know that?"

"Fair point."

We cross the road, and I pick up my pace to keep up with Gray's long strides. "Tell me about this new mistress. I missed that part."

"She is an actress."

KELLEY ARMSTRONG

"Ah."

That's all that really needs to be said. Female actors inhabit an odd place in Victorian society. They're independent women pursuing a career that was once entirely the province of men.

Actresses have more freedom than the average Victorian woman. Yet when women move out of their prescribed roles, they risk no longer being seen as "proper women." They become dangerous, and the easiest way to dismiss them is to question their morals.

To many, "actress" means "harlot." They are considered women of easy virtue who make most of their living off the stage. Do some of them engage in sex work? Sure. So do some shop girls and factory workers. Mostly, actresses just enjoy a greater freedom overall, which also extends to their sex lives.

"Did Arthur give you a name for this actress?" I ask.

"He did. I do not recognize it, and he says she's an ingenue."

"Young, then."

"Catriona's age or slightly older."

While a nonmonogamous arrangement wouldn't be my choice, it *is* a valid choice. With Lady Inglis and Lord Simpson, not only are both parties consenting, but both parties apparently pursue other relationships. So maybe it shouldn't bother me that Simpson is hooking up with an actress half Lady Inglis's age. But it does because I can't help but wonder whether it would also bother Lady Inglis.

Sharing him with other mature widows would be one thing. This feels... It feels like the stereotypical form of adultery, the guy screwing around with a girl from a lower social strata, one young enough to be his daughter.

SCHEMES & SCANDALS

If Lady Inglis *is* bothered, might she decide she'd finally had enough of this open relationship and lock him in with marriage? She *did* visit just before the letters went missing.

I'm not sure how I feel about Lady Inglis—and I know any judgment could be marred by her past with Gray—but I'd like her to be what she seems to be: a merry widow, independent, free thinking and free loving, not an aging woman who fears losing her lover to a younger woman and tricks him into marrying her.

I don't say any of that to Gray. Arthur Simpson raised the possibility, and I will let Gray bring it up. If he doesn't, then I trust his judgment.

"Could the actress be a suspect?" I say. "She might be the hot young new fling, but Lady Inglis is the longtime lover who'd stand in the way of the actress winning Lord Simpson." I pause. "Is that even a possibility? Can an actress marry a lord?"

"It has happened," he says. "More likely, though, there would be an arrangement."

Like what the woman earlier thought I'd been seeking with Arthur Simpson. A sugar daddy.

"However," Gray says, "you are forgetting that the actress could not have stolen the letters. She spent the night *before* they disappeared."

"Which only means she could have found them while she was there and then snuck back to steal them."

He sighs. "I did not think of that."

"This is why you're the junior detective. But don't worry. You'll get the hang of it someday."

Eleven

EXT ON our interview list is the valet. He'd said he wanted to spend the holidays home with his family, but when we knock on his sister's door, she tells us he's working at a pub.

"Poor lad cannot even take the holidays off," she says. "That man let him go without a penny's wages. At this time of year? Can you believe it?"

That certainly isn't the story Lord Simpson gave, and it seems odd that he'd send us after the valet with a lie easily exposed.

She gives us directions to the pub, and then says, "Tell Lewis he need not bring home any money for the rent. I know he feels he must contribute, but I do not begrudge him a few coins in his pocket."

I ask for a description of her brother, and she seems confused—why do we need that when he's working there, easily found? Still, she describes him, and we set off along the snowy streets.

Along the way, we pass a small market, and I slow to eye the wares. It seems to be a little holiday market, full of holiday

KELLEY ARMSTRONG

purchases—a stall of sweets, another of toys, a third of toiletries wrapped in pretty bows.

"Have you finished your Hogmanay shopping yet?" Gray asks.

"Isla and I went out last week, but I couldn't buy for her, obviously." I didn't buy for him, either, as I continue mulling over and rejecting ideas. Gray is fond of giving me gifts—perfect little presents that only I would appreciate, like a poison ring or a tiny derringer. I need to get exactly the right one for him.

"Do you wish to pause here?" he says. "Find something for her?"

My gaze slides over the stalls. I have a few ideas, but like buying for Gray, I won't find the right gift for Isla here. I still take the excuse to wander and browse. I purchase scented hair oil for Simon, and Gray buys a bag of boiled sweets for Alice, mostly so two of the best-dressed customers don't walk away without spending any money.

"Where do you shop for presents in your time?" Gray asks as we continue on.

"Online."

He gives me a look.

I shrug. "I'm not much of a shopper. I know what I want, and I order it online and get it shipped to my door."

"That sounds…"

"Soulless?"

"I was going to say wonderfully convenient." He slides a glance my way. "I do not suppose I can hope for such things in my lifetime?"

"It only started in *my* lifetime." I peer in the sooty window of a curiosities shop. "I do like to go out at least once for actual holiday shopping. When I was visiting my nan a few years back, she took me to the Christmas market here."

SCHEMES & SCANDALS

"A Christmas market in Edinburgh? Sacrilege."

I smile. "They still do a big blowout for Hogmanay. Music, live theater, and lots of fireworks." I glance at him. "You have fireworks, right?"

One brow shoots up.

"Don't give me that look," I say. "I know they were invented in China centuries ago, but I don't know when they arrived in the UK. I'm not a historian."

"Have you heard of Guy Fawkes?"

"Right! Bonfire night. *Remember, remember, the fifth of November.* Mostly by blowing things up. Including fireworks, in honor of foiling Fawkes's plan to blow up parliament. When did that happen? About fifty years ago?"

"1605."

"Huh. History. Really not my thing."

"Evidently. Yes, we have Gunpowder Treason Day, which can be celebrated with bonfires and fireworks. In fact, until about ten years ago, it was illegal not to celebrate it."

I peer at him.

"The Observance of Fifth November Act," he says. "It was repealed in the past decade."

I can't tell whether he's serious. Before I can ask more, we arrive at the pub. It's a tavern in a middling area of the Old Town. Very small, very dark, very much a local watering hole. At this time of day—early afternoon—it's only about half full.

Using the description Lewis's sister gave, it's easy enough to find the valet, being the only guy under forty. He's deep in conversation with an older man, and unless his "job" involves

KELLEY ARMSTRONG

chatting up customers while downing a pint himself, he is not working.

Here's another interesting thing about Victorian life. When I see depictions of domestic staff, they look very proper, like poor relations of the family they serve. Diffident, polite, starched, even a little stuffy. If I could picture their home lives, I'd see them sitting by the fire stitching Bible verses into tea towels. The truth is, of course, that their work persona is an act. Or, more accurately, it's Victorian code-switching. They act and talk in a manner that reflects well on their employers. Get them away from work, and it's very different.

Gray doesn't have a valet, but I've met a few, and they are very dapper and proper soft-spoken men. That is not the guy downing that pint. He's loud, gesturing wildly, and unshaven in a way that suggests he just hasn't bothered with it in a few days. He's young—maybe midtwenties—and handsome, and I can tell he'd clean up well enough to present the very picture of a fashionable young valet. Right now, though, he's off the clock. Permanently off the clock.

As we move toward Lewis, he glances over. Then he stops midsentence, stares at Gray for a moment, drops his pint and runs.

I look at Gray, who looks at me.

"That was...unexpected," Gray says. "I suppose we should go after him."

"Nah, we can just grab a drink. He'll be back soon enough." I smile at Gray's obvious disappointment. "Yes, we're going after him."

SCHEMES & SCANDALS

I LET GRAY give chase out the back door as I head around front. It's the Old Town, but it's a decent neighborhood and midday. I'm not concerned about being alone—either for safety or propriety.

I slip out the front and look each way. Like many streets in the Old Town, it's so narrow that two coaches can't pass each other. These are medieval roads, meant for walking and riding horses and maybe pulling a cart. At midday, the street is crowded, and I scan for Lewis's light hair. He hadn't bothered to grab his outerwear when he ran, which should make him easier to spot. There's no sign of him, though.

The rear door would likely exit into a close—an even narrower lane between buildings, similar to an alley. I hurry left, spot a close and pick up my pace. I swing into it to find an exceptionally narrow passage. Towering buildings on both sides plunge the alley into darkness. I break into a slow jog as I strain to listen. Somewhere ahead, I catch the pound of running feet.

A rickety wooden staircase blocks easy passage. That's not unusual. Access to many apartment floors requires external stairs so decrepit they make me shudder. I duck past this set and—

A figure grabs me from the shadows. I wheel, fists rising, only to stop when I catch a glimpse of a tall man in a fur-trimmed coat and top hat.

"Goddamn it," I say. "How many times do I need to warn you not to sneak…"

I trail off as I squint up into the pale face of a stranger.

"Well, now, you have a tongue on you, don't you, lass?"

KELLEY ARMSTRONG

The man is about Gray's age and height, but otherwise, there's no way to mistake one for the other. He's missing half his teeth, and a dentist would insist on pulling the remainder. Even his coat only superficially resembles Gray's. It's shabby and tattered, and the smell of it is enough to have me backpedaling even as his grip tightens on my arm.

"What a fine little thing you are," he says, with a wave of breath that smells worse than a week-old corpse. "Such fancy clothing. Surely you can spare a few coins for my supper, lass?"

I eye him, thinking fast. When he calls me "fine," he means my clothing, which indicates I have a bit of money. That's what he's interested in. While I'm carrying a derringer in my cloak pocket and a knife in my boot, I'd rather not pull them if I can part with a few coins instead. The last time I stabbed a man who grabbed me in an alley, I spent the night in jail for assault.

"I am sorry, sir," I say with a pretty half curtsy. "I mistook you for another. Yes, I believe I can spare a few pence to help a gentleman down on his luck. God tells us to be charitable."

I cast my gaze up in what I hope is a pious expression as I fish a few coins from my pocket. When I extend my hand, I see I'm offering three pence and two shillings. More than I intended, but not more than I'm willing to give.

"If you will please remove your hand from my arm, sir," I say. "Your grip is very tight."

He tightens it enough to make me inhale sharply.

"Is that better?" he says.

"I am offering you money, sir," I say, struggling to keep my voice sweet and a little confused. "That is what you asked for."

SCHEMES & SCANDALS

"It's not enough."

I look down at my hand to double-check the coins. Hell, yes, it's enough. From Gray and Isla, I've learned more about charity than I knew in modern-day Vancouver, where I'd walk past panhandlers with an "I don't see you" expression and make a mental note to donate to a shelter instead. Here, a few small coins go a long way. What I'm offering is double what he should expect.

"Forgive me, sir," I say, "but I need my last shilling to get home again."

"You can walk. You'll give me that last shilling…and everything else in your pockets, along with that ring on your finger and the necklace—"

"There you are," a voice rumbles behind us. "I wondered where the devil you took off to."

I turn to see Gray and bow my head. "I am sorry, sir. I tried to take a shortcut."

He grunts. "And look where that got you." He lifts his gaze to the man still holding my arm. "I am going to presume you are holding my assistant's arm because you helped her up from an unfortunate fall."

The man's gaze sweeps up Gray and back down, his eyes narrowing as he assesses. Then he says, "If I did, I believe I am due some recompense. Who knows what could have befallen the child back here."

Gray hands him a shilling. "There. Thank you for your kindness."

The man looks at me, that narrow-eyed gaze telling me I still owe him the money I offered.

KELLEY ARMSTRONG

"How generous, sir," I say to Gray. "I was about to pay this good man myself, but as you have done so, I will take my leave of him." I look at the fingers gripping on my arm. "I am quite recovered, sir. You may remove your hand."

The man hesitates. Gray tenses, jaw setting, and with another look at him, the man releases my arm, mutters something and disappears into the shadows again.

Gray ushers me along the alley, and I mutter, "Do not do that."

"Do not do what? Rescue you from ruffians twice your size?"

I snort. "He was just a troll, guarding his bridge and demanding a fare for passage."

"Which you had offered, and he was not accepting."

"I was working it out."

Gray looks down at me.

"You need to let me work it out, Duncan," I say, my voice softer. "I do appreciate that you were close enough to intercede. If I hadn't been able to get out of it, I'd also have appreciated actual intercession. But I need to find strategies for all situations in this world."

"What would you have done in yours?"

I consider as we step onto another street. "If he'd just asked, I'd have given him money. Grabbing my arm changes things. That's a threat. I'd have shown him not to expect women to be easy marks."

"And you would not do that in this world?"

I turn a look on him. "Remember why I spent a night in jail this spring? Also, knocking him down is a whole lot harder in this body and this clothing."

"All right. So I should watch until you need my help? Presumably signaling to you that I am near."

SCHEMES & SCANDALS

"Mmm. Signaling me means I know I have backup, which changes things, but sure. Signal me and then stand down until the last possible moment."

"The split second between him pulling out a knife and ramming it between your ribs?"

"Pfft. I'm wearing a cloak, dress, corset cover, and corset. He'd better have a sharp knife and a sharper sense of anatomy."

Gray sighs and steers me around a woman passed out drunk.

"I'm guessing we lost Lewis?" I say.

"No."

Gray leads me down another close, this one wider and busier, with people walking in both directions. Then he pauses and points with his chin. Ahead is a recessed doorway, and in it stands Lewis, pressed against the rear as if rendered invisible.

Now it's my turn to sigh. Yes, household staff might not be as prim and proper as they appear on the job, but unless they work for Isla Ballantyne, they're not exactly criminal geniuses, either.

"Head around and come in the other way," I say. "I'll wait here. When I see you, I'll approach him. Be ready in case he runs."

"Is that an order?" he says.

"Of course. I'm the lead detective, remember?"

His headshake says he's humoring me, but he does backtrack the way he came. That means I need a reason for hanging out here that doesn't look like active solicitation. That isn't easy with Catriona's body and a lack of "pause in public place" excuses like cell phones.

I decide to fuss with my glove. Pull it off. Peer inside, scowling slightly, as if something is poking at me. I'm turning each finger

KELLEY ARMSTRONG

inside out when I finally spot Gray. He slips into the end of the close, sees me, and then moves to the side and removes his own glove to examine it.

I laugh softly at that and put my glove on before someone decides we're engaged in an elaborate mating ritual. Or planning a midday heist.

I stroll over to where Lewis still "hides" in the recessed doorway.

"Hello, Lewis," I say.

He frowns at me with zero recognition. Apparently, the only one he saw at the pub was Gray.

"I need to speak to you about Lord Simpson," I say. "We had your sister's address and—"

Lewis flinches, his gaze going over my shoulder. I look to see Gray.

"He's with me," I say.

Lewis looks from Gray to me and says, "Lord Simpson sent you?"

"No, but we're here investigating his missing property."

"This has nothing to do with, er, a young lady I've been seeing?"

"Uh...no."

Lewis exhales. "I thought it was about that. She has an older brother, and they are… That is to say, he might resemble…"

He trails off, but I can figure out the rest. Lewis is seeing a young woman of color, and on seeing a man of color bearing down on him, he bolted.

"This has nothing to do with your social life," I say. "It is entirely about work. Speaking of which, though, your sister seems to think you're employed at that pub."

SCHEMES & SCANDALS

His eyes open, far too wide to be genuine shock. "What? No. She must have misunderstood."

"She says Lord Simpson let you go without a shilling in payment, when he told us he paid you a quarter's wages."

Lewis colors and tugs at his collar. "She's misunderstood."

In other words, Simpson did pay, but Lewis doesn't want his sister knowing he has money. He's pretending to work at the pub and then giving her a few "hard-earned" coins for his rent, like a good brother.

This puts us in a position of power. If he decides not to cooperate with the interview, we have leverage.

"No matter," I say. "We are here to speak of Lord Simpson's missing property. Would you like to go someplace else?"

"I am a wee bit thirsty," he says, "from all the running."

"Let us return to your pub and buy you a pint."

Twelve

YEP. GOTTA love Victorian detective work, where even McCreadie wouldn't see a problem interviewing a witness over a pint. We get Lewis settled in with a fresh drink, and Gray takes one for himself, to be hospitable. I'm tempted to ask for a glass of water, but... there's a reason why beer is so popular in historical times. It's not that everyone was a lush, downing a "small beer" with breakfast, giving beer to children and such. It's that beer—or cider or wine—is safe to drink where water might not be. Boiling it for tea helps, but I won't find tea here, so I settle on a small glass of beer. While the beer itself might be safe, I can't say as much for the smudged glass. Welcome to the time before running hot water and cheap soap.

"I know about the missing letters from Lady Inglis," he says. "Lord Simpson came and spoke to me."

I hesitate. "He told you they were from Lady Inglis?"

"No, but I cannot see his other mistresses penning him letters, and I know he's been receiving them since he hired me, so they

KELLEY ARMSTRONG

must be from Lady Inglis. A fine lady, that one. He really ought to marry her."

"So we've heard," I murmur.

"I can understand him liking the actresses and such, but I do not get the sense Lady Inglis would mind if he continued that, discreetly, of course. She is a very sensible lady. And that house could use a mistress."

"Has Lady Inglis indicated she'd like the position?"

"As lady of the house? No. She teases him about its management, and he says she's welcome to do it for him, but she says she has her own household to manage. The solution, clearly, is to marry. Her house is much nicer, and they could boot out that sodding brother of his."

I press more. I really do want to know whether Lady Inglis has given any sense that she's unhappy with the arrangement or would like to marry Lord Simpson. Lewis has seen none of that.

So why should she want to marry a man of equal rank, with a lesser home, a loutish brother, and multiple mistresses? The question confuses Lewis. She's a woman without a man. Of course she must secretly wish to marry.

This is one of the things that astounds me about the Victorian male. How he can see a woman enjoying an independent life and say, "That poor dear, if only she had a man." It's not just men, either. Older women say the same thing. Of course, the older women who say it are all married and may just not want other women having things they do not.

I conclude that Lady Inglis has given zero indication of wanting to marry Lord Simpson. Lewis just thinks she should, for the

SCHEMES & SCANDALS

convenience of his former employer, who is in need of a good domestic manager.

"You seem fond of Lord Simpson," I say. "It was an amicable parting?"

Lewis shrugs. "I would have preferred *not* to have been sacked, but his lordship assured me I will receive excellent references. Apparently, Lord Simpson did not think I would do well overseas, and while I would have appreciated the chance to prove otherwise, that is his choice, and he paid me well."

I glance at Gray. I'm asking whether he wishes to continue this line of questioning, but he only uses it as an opportunity to swing the interview back to the stolen goods.

"So you knew of the letters," Gray says.

"Yes, sir. And if you are going to ask whether I took them, I almost wish I had."

Gray frowns.

Lewis gives a low laugh and leans back in his chair. "I'd be a wealthy man if I did. Wealthy enough, that is. Seems very unfair, if you ask me. Had I stolen from his lordship, I'd be buying passage on a ship to America with a pocket full of money to make my fortune there. But no, I was an honest chap, and so I have nothing." Lewis shifts in his seat. "All right, his lordship *did* give me a few quid for my honesty, but it's a sad world when a man would have gained more for admitting he was a thief."

"I…do not understand," Gray says.

"Lord Simpson says whoever stole the letters wants money for their return. He offered me five *hundred* quid to quietly return the letters. Alas, being an honest man, I could not claim it."

KELLEY ARMSTRONG

Lewis sips his beer and continues, "I even thought perhaps I could say I stole the letters and burned them, but he required the return of the letters." He shakes his head. "That will teach me to be honest."

I see Lewis's point, even if he is belaboring it. Simpson meant well, but his execution was flawed.

Could Lewis still have stolen the letters? Maybe he knew Simpson had no intention of paying and just wanted a confession so he could put the screws to his former valet and get those letters back for free. Or Lewis could be playing it safe and waiting for the payout. Except the payout isn't actually the safe bet here because if Lady Inglis decides not to give in to the blackmail, he's stuck with the much smaller reward of income from publishing the letters.

Lewis doesn't strike me as a guy who'd think through all the angles. If he stole the letters and Simpson showed up on his doorstep, he'd freak out. If Simpson offered to pay the full amount of the blackmail, he'd jump at it.

Also, Simpson doesn't strike me as someone who'd offer money and then replace it with threats. No, I suspect Simpson really would try to buy back those letters, and if Lewis had them, he'd hand them over.

After we wrap up the interview, I run this all past Gray, who agrees with my logic. Lewis hardly seems like a wily blackmailer. And the Lord Simpson Gray knows isn't going to get a confession and then refuse to pay.

Lewis isn't a vengeful former employee. He's a guy who has been let go but paid well for the inconvenience. He'll spend his

SCHEMES & SCANDALS

holidays drinking and seeing his girlfriend and then, in the new year, he'll take Simpson up on that offer of references to get a new job.

That clears our most obvious suspect.

I'M SPENDING THE evening alone. Gray is paying a house call to a family too illustrious to make funeral arrangements in an undertaker's office. While I'm technically his assistant, I can't yet pass as a Victorian well enough to be sure I won't say or do something wrong in front of grieving families. It's easy to explain away my peccadilloes in everyday life. Dealing with the grief-stricken is another level, one where I want my manners to be perfect.

Isla is out on a social call. She has two sorts of social engagements. One is lunches and teas and such with women whose company she genuinely enjoys. The other is duty, all the various charitable endeavors that women like Isla are expected to engage in.

Those charitable endeavors would seem like a happy duty for Isla, who is genuinely interested in the plight of the poor. Unfortunately, in those settings, she's one of the very few *genuinely* interested women.

We're at a time of shifting views on the poor and charity. My father used to teach this with Dickens in particular, showing how Dickens's own views shifted over the course of his career. He moved from heartily endorsing charity from the rich to questioning whether it can ever *not* be condescending, while advocating

KELLEY ARMSTRONG

for other solutions. That's the dilemma Isla faces—she wants to use her privilege to help, but is it ever possible to do that, however sincerely, without condescension?

With both of them gone, I am alone and reminded that, since I have decided to stay in this world, I really need to make a full life for myself here, including hobbies. Normally, I would see whether Alice wanted to play cards, but she's with Mrs. Wallace, and I don't dare intrude.

Alice and Mrs. Wallace are enjoying a free evening with both Isla and Gray away. Our bosses might be very low maintenance, but as long as they're in the house, the staff is on alert, ready at the sound of footsteps to see whether anything is needed. With both Gray and Isla gone, Alice and Mrs. Wallace can truly relax.

My other option is to pop out to the stables for a chat with Simon, which is always time well spent. He was Catriona's only real friend, and while I can't fill that role, I very much enjoy his company. However, he is with Gray, who can't be seen paying visits to clients on foot.

That leaves me with reading, which would usually be fine, but reading reminds me of Dickens, which reminds me that I met a dead man two days ago.

I'm struggling with that more than I would have expected. Last month, I watched my terminally ill grandmother die, but it's not the same. I met a man who believes himself to be healthy, who is on his last tour before settling into semiretirement. I listened to a man enthuse about a book he will never finish writing. It has unsettled me more than I expected, and I realize some of my

SCHEMES & SCANDALS

earlier pique with Gray might be misdirected emotional fallout from that.

When I first came to this world, I'd felt lonely in a way I didn't even truly recognize as loneliness.

Now Gray, Isla, and McCreadie all know my secret, and with that, I have friends I can be myself around. Yet I have given them a secret *they* must keep, and I don't want to add to that with the uncomfortable sort of prognostication that comes with realizing someone is going to die.

But keeping that secret lets the loneliness creep in again, along with the fear that I'm always going to be an outsider, however much they welcome me. There will always be knowledge—uncomfortable knowledge—that I can't share.

So when Jack swings into the library, I may greet her a wee bit more effusively than normal.

"Bored, are you?" she says, tugging at her trousers as if she just finished changing into her male garb.

I shrug. "A bit out of sorts. What are you up to tonight?"

"And can you join? That is your real question."

Another shrug as I play it cool. "Depends on what it is and whether you want company."

"From the look you gave when I walked in, unless I plan to spend the night digging through rubbish, you'll think it sounds splendid."

"You can find a lot of interesting things in the rubbish."

She laughs. "The situation is desperate, then. Well, I came to see whether you'd care to call on a print shop. To learn whether anyone might be offering letters of an intimate nature for paid public consumption?"

KELLEY ARMSTRONG

"Ah. That *does* sound more interesting than picking through rubbish."

"We can stop for a pint afterwards," she says. "You can be my lady friend for the evening."

"Which means you'll be paying for the pint? Excellent."

Thirteen

ACK IS the sort of person who lets you feel as if you know them, but once you stop to think about it, you realize you don't know a damn thing. She's chatty and open, and gives the impression that she likes you, and that you could be friends...or at least friendly acquaintances. But she has perfected the art of talking a great deal without giving away one iota of truly personal information.

I don't know how old she is, where she grew up, what sort of life she's had, what her plans for the future are or her pains of the past. She could come from poverty or royalty. She could have two husbands and a child growing up with relatives. She seems like someone who has waltzed through life, spinning too deftly for anything to leave a scar. Maybe that's true. Maybe it's a persona she adopts, like the masculine one she's inhabiting as we cross the mound into the Old Town.

I am fascinated by Jack, and I'm also learning from her, even if she never realizes it. How she acts is how I must act toward most of the world...including her. My past isn't something I can

KELLEY ARMSTRONG

discuss, both because it took place over a century from now and because I'm inhabiting the body of someone who already has a past. What if I tell Simon that my parents were loving and incredibly supportive, only to have him remember that Catriona's were cold or abusive?

I've never been a private person. Hell, meet me at a party and you'd walk away an hour later knowing my favorite color, the name of my childhood cat, and that I broke my arm in third grade, climbing a tree. Yes, I broke it climbing a tree, not falling from it, which is a certain kind of special.

On the walk, Jack chatters away. She tells me something funny Alice said and how Mrs. Wallace gave her shit for whistling, which she relates in a perfect imitation of the housekeeper. She points out a Princes Street shop that kicked her out last year when she'd been browsing "intimate ladies' apparel" while forgetting she was still dressed masculine. Once we're in the Old Town, she points out a close and tells me a friend swears it's haunted by one of Burke and Hare's victims. All very entertaining and companionable, and not revealing one scrap of personal insight.

"Did you grow up in Edinburgh?" I say, mostly just to amuse myself because I know how she'll answer.

"Here and there, now and then." She waves a hand. "You know how it is. You?"

"Same."

She shoots me a grin, as if she knows I'm playing her game. She's said many times that she knows something's up with me, some secret she's not privy to. That would make me nervous if I got the sense she was digging for answers. After all, she *is* a

SCHEMES & SCANDALS

journalist, by practice if not by trade. But my sense is that this is a secret she'll let me keep, as long as I let her keep all of hers, which seems fair.

It's a clear night, crisp and decently lit with stars just visible through the smoke of a thousand fires keeping a thousand lodgings warm—or warm enough. We weave through a few neighborhoods before she slows.

"Here we are," she says.

I look around, but I'm not even sure I recognize the area. She leads me to a building with no obvious storefront…and no obvious front door. We go to the side entrance, and she raps a few times in a pattern.

"Secret entry code," I say, and then stop myself before adding a period-inappropriate "Cool."

A moment later, there's a snick, and I notice a peephole on the solid door. Another moment passes, and a lock clangs. Then the door opens a few inches, and the unmistakable smell of ink rushes out.

"You have something for me, boy?" a voice rumbles.

"Questions," Jack says cheerfully. "I have questions."

The door slams shut. Jack only sighs and knocks again. When it opens, it's a scant inch, and the voice rumbles, "You come here with a stranger and questions? You're lucky I don't set Blackie on you."

"Have you seen these?" Jack waves one of the pamphlet installments of Gray's adventures. "I have it on good authority that the scribe is looking to change presses."

There's a pause. It's long enough that I'm concerned, but Jack only waits.

KELLEY ARMSTRONG

"You know the writer?" the voice says.

"Would you like a peek at the next installment to prove it?"

More silence. The peephole snicks open again.

"Miss Mallory?" the voice says.

Thankfully, I don't jump, though I will give Jack shit for not warning me. Or actually, maybe I won't, because she probably thought I'd figure it out as soon as she waved around that pamphlet.

"Yes, the pamphlet is about the adventures of Dr. Gray and his lovely assistant, Miss Mallory," Jack says breezily.

"I mean, is that Miss Mallory with you?"

Jack looks over at me and blinks, as if in surprise. Then she laughs. "Heavens, no. Miss Mallory with me? A pleasant thought. She sounds a right perfect little morsel. This one is a right perfect pain in the arse."

I'm allowed to glare at her for that, and I do, but the door also opens to let us in, as if the person on the other side suspects I'm "Miss Mallory," but they aren't pushing for a positive ID.

The door opens into darkness. We slip inside, and I see the owner of the voice, a stout woman with her arms crossed over her chest. I glance around for the dog, Blackie, and instead see a hulking guy with jet-black hair and an equally black beard, his arms also crossed. The woman leads us past him, and I swear he growls… until I look up at him from under my lashes. Then his broad face colors, and he tips his grimy hat with a few mumbled words.

The woman takes us into what is obviously the print room, given the two printing presses. That's where my attention goes: to those presses.

SCHEMES & SCANDALS

My parents talk of their childhoods, with no computers, just typewriters and mimeograph machines, and that's always been hard for me to fathom. How do you write an essay if you can't just pull up the file and edit it into submission? What if you need more than one copy? You couldn't even go to the library and use the copy machine.

I remember once when they were explaining these concepts to me, and I blurted, "But what about books?" How did you produce a thousand copies of a book without printers? Did they live back in that time I'd seen in old movies, with massive printing presses and movable type? They'd thought that was hilarious…and then gently explained all the steps between ancient printing presses and modern ones.

Here, I expect to see one of those massive beasts that would take up an entire room. Instead, there are two presses. Both are much smaller than I expected, maybe double the size of those old library copy machines from my youth.

The room is cavernous, and I see what looks like living quarters to one side. The rest is boxes. Some seem to be finished products, and I squint into one and see flyers for a workers' rights movement. And in the one beside it…fancy pamphlets arguing *against* the dangers of granting workers more rights.

"Your friend there should keep her eyes to herself," the woman rumbles.

"Occupational hazard," I say with a smile, mostly to watch her pause to decipher that very modern phrase. When she does, she eyes me. "You really are Miss Mallory, then? Of the stories?"

"Miss Mallory is sweet and gentle," Jack says. "And knows not to poke her nose where it doesn't belong."

KELLEY ARMSTRONG

It's a credit to her acting ability that she can say that with a straight face.

"I am only fascinated by the presses," I say. "May I ask why there are two?"

The woman sighs, as if I'm being unreasonably curious, but her eyes light with the look of someone who actually likes talking about her work. The smaller machine is a jobbing press meant for simple low-print tasks like letterhead or business cards. It takes about fifteen minutes to set up and can print a thousand copies an hour. The larger one is the proper press and can do about half as many copies an hour. Both are manual presses. Newspapers use steam-powered ones, which can do about ten thousand pages an hour, but her business has no need for that.

I cut my questions short at Jack's obvious impatience, and then she says, "I come tonight with questions about pornographic literature."

The woman eyes me again. "If you're not Miss Mallory and you're looking for a few extra coins in your pocket, I can suggest an artist or two. Sketches are best. Photographs do not flatter as well."

"And if I *am* Miss Mallory, and I were still looking to make a few extra coins? Would your answer be something different?"

"In that case, it would. I'd suggest your chronicler print a separate set of your adventures…for a different but better-paying sort of customer."

I smile and shake my head. "I can imagine the poor mother who picks up the wrong one to share with her children. No, in either case, I am not looking for that sort of extra coin. I merely accompany Jack on his labors tonight."

SCHEMES & SCANDALS

"His labors being the pursuit of pornographic literature?" she says.

"*Questions* about pornographic literature," Jack says as she lifts a chapbook from a box. "Like this."

The woman sniffs. "You do not want that. It is far too pretty for a young man like you. That sort of thing is written for Miss Not-Mallory over here."

I take the chapbook from Jack. It's only about twenty pages long. On a skim, I can see it's a story about a young woman alone in the city, innocent and sweet. By page five, she's no longer so innocent and sweet.

I wrinkle my nose. "This is written for men."

Jack's and the printer's brows shoot up in unison.

I wave the chapbook. "Innocent girl. Big bad city. Oh, please don't touch me there. No, wait, I like being touched there. There would be a female audience for it, but it's mostly aimed at men."

"We have others," the printer says.

"Such as?"

"Not-so-innocent governess who goes to work for a lord and his longtime friend."

"Is the friend actually just a friend?"

She meets my gaze. "No."

"Huh. That might work. The key is the not-so-innocent part. Women don't want to read about other women being ruined. They want to read about them having fun."

Jack chokes on a laugh.

The printer says, "We also have an entire series called The Merry Widow."

KELLEY ARMSTRONG

That makes me think of Lady Inglis, but I hide my reaction. "Even better."

"The Merry Widow, you say?" Jack murmurs, moving forward. "So there is an appetite for such things?"

"The fellow who has them printed up certainly seems to think so."

"And if someone came by asking about printing intimate letters written by an actual widow, you'd send them to him?"

She waves a hand. "No, it's not that sort of thing. This fellow has a writer already. And they aren't letters. They're stories."

"So if I had such letters…?" Jack says.

She snorts. "Keep them." Her eyes glitter. "Unless they were written by that most illustrious of widows. Adventures between her illustrious self and a certain Scottish servant?"

It takes a moment to realize she means Queen Victoria, and even I flush at that. I do recall the widowed queen was rumored to have an affair with a Scotsman who worked on her estate.

Jack rolls her eyes. "If I had those, I'd be a rich man. One such letter from Her Royal Highness, and my coffers would fill in the blink of an eye."

"Or you'd wind up in the dungeons," the printer says. "Never to be seen or heard from again."

"True enough. But what if the letters were from a less illustrious personage?"

The printer shrugs. "If she has money and you took the letters without permission, you'd make far more by asking her to pay to *prevent* them from being printed."

That gives me pause. "Do such things happen?" I ask.

126

SCHEMES & SCANDALS

"I'm certain they do. It does not involve me, though."

"So if I brought you such letters, you would not print them?"

She meets my gaze. "I would not."

"Would you know anyone who would?"

She shrugs. "A shop or two, but they'd only buy them for a few pounds, and then probably turn around and see if they could 'sell' them back to the writer. Why print such things written by amateurs when you can have them written by experts?"

"Experts using the full scope of their imaginations," I say. "Rather than relying on fact."

The printer points an ink-blackened finger at me. "Just so. I do not think you are going to find many merry widows with the temerity and the skill to write of their intimate adventures, and even if they did, they would not sell as well as the made-up sort."

Jack asks a few more questions, but it's clear that the printer hasn't heard of anyone trying to sell such letters. From what I gather, this shop would be their first stop, as it's well known for its underground publications. But the printer is correct, too, that no one is likely to print such a thing when the real money would be made in blackmailing the letter writer.

As we prepare to leave, I say, "You mentioned a Merry Widow series. Might I purchase those?"

The printer gives a low, rumbling laugh. "Caught your fancy, did they?"

"They did."

"Well, I am only the printer, but I have some samples I'd be willing to part with for a few shillings. Do you want the governess one as well?"

KELLEY ARMSTRONG

I imagine Isla reading that story, with the governess, the lord, and his more-than-a-friend. "No, the Merry Widow ones will suffice."

"Well, I shall throw that one in as an extra." She winks. "You might find it more to your taste than you would expect."

I make my purchase, and we leave. We don't get more than a few feet from the shop before Jack says to me, in her more natural voice, "Getting a little lonely in that attic bedroom, is it?"

I make a noncommittal noise. I'm certainly not telling her who they're for. Also, I probably *will* need to read them to make sure I'm not giving Isla anything so far out of her comfort zone that she might never recover.

"You do know there is an easy fix for that," she says. "A mere two flights down. A very fine doctor who would happily provide whatever examination you require."

I can feel her gaze on me in the dark, waiting for a reaction. I only shake my head. "If you mean our shared employer, that is inappropriate."

She makes a rude noise. "Not unless you only agree because he *is* your employer. Otherwise, it is a perfectly fine arrangement." She glances over. "It adds quite an exciting dynamic, as I say from experience."

"I thought all your experiences were neither exciting nor dynamic."

"Mmm, I will not say that one was excellent, but it was the best of the bunch. He was my first employer. First *legitimate* employer, that is." She grins my way. "I had taken the position posing as a boy, which only added to the illicit allure. He enjoyed knowing my little secret and being the only one to see me in a dress." She

SCHEMES & SCANDALS

purses her lips. "Though there was that one time when he did not want me to change into a dress first."

She peers at me and sighs. "You are quite impossible to shock, Miss Mallory."

"Not really. You just need to tell me something shocking. Like that he invited three of his friends along for the ride."

Her cheeks redden, and I laugh.

She scowls at me. "You enjoyed that."

"You started it. Do not try to shock me in such regards, my dear, or I shall turn the tables faster than you like. Now, you promised me a pint, did you not?"

"I just helped you with your case. And helped you find reading material. I think you owe *me* a pint."

"True, however, if you choose to dress as a lad, you must behave as a lad. It would not do for people to see a young lady paying for your pint. What would they think?"

She shakes her head and grumbles under her breath as she leads me to a pub.

Fourteen

WHEN WE get back to the town house, the coach has returned, and we pop into the stable to speak to Simon, who's putting Folly to bed for the night. Simon has been wary around Jack. It isn't that he has an issue with cross-dressing. That's actually why Isla hired him. Simon was part of the molly subculture, as a gay man who sometimes socialized while dressed as a woman. He'd been young, and with youth can come the confidence that people won't care what you do as long as it doesn't hurt them. A lovely sentiment, but sadly false.

While being a gay man isn't illegal in Scotland, as it is elsewhere in Britain, it's still not something you want to flaunt, which is what got Simon into trouble. If he's cautious around Jack, it's because she's cross-dressing for a different reason. Tonight, though, they strike up a conversation, and I use the opportunity to slip off and give them a chance to chat.

I'm just inside the door and sitting to change into my indoor footwear when boots clomp on the stairs. I look up to see Gray coming down.

KELLEY ARMSTRONG

"You were out," he says.

I lift the winter boot I just removed. "Yes."

"It is late."

"It is." I finish lacing my indoor boots. While I'm going to need to take them off again upstairs in my room, walking around in my stocking feet would be like walking around half dressed. It is simply not done.

I stand. "I did leave a note."

"Yes, I got it."

I lean against the wall and look up at him still halfway down the stairs. "You know, this feels familiar. Like when I was a teenager and I'd come home past curfew and my dad would wait up to give me hell."

"I did not wait up. I was *still* up."

I don't answer that. I know from Simon that Gray has been home for the past hour, and given how late it is, he'd normally have gone straight to his room.

"But you *are* giving me hell?" I say.

"I am expressing mild concern. I know you were with Jack, and I know you are fond of her, but I am not convinced…"

"She wouldn't leave me to my fate if we got jumped in an alley?"

"Exactly so."

"I had my gun and my knife."

He considers this. Not considering whether this is enough—I suspect I could roll through the Old Town in a tank and he still wouldn't be convinced it was safe enough. What he's considering is whether he would be justified in pursuing the complaint.

132

SCHEMES & SCANDALS

"How was *your* evening?" I ask.

He still pauses, as if debating whether he's ready to drop this. Then he sighs. "It went much later than I expected. I thought I would have been done hours ago, but I was not even granted an audience until nearly nine."

"Damned nobility."

"I considered leaving. Unfortunately, they were good clients of my father's, and they are also well connected enough that being rude to them might cost me half my clientele. Which sometimes I think would not be the worst thing..." He scratches his chin and sighs again. "Perhaps someday."

I used to wonder why Gray keeps the undertaking business when he clearly does not care for it...and doesn't need the money. I understand better now. It's duty and pride. Duty to his family, because his father built the business and Gray inherited it. It's also pride because his forensic work doesn't pay the bills, and he wouldn't be comfortable living off passive income from money his father made and invested.

"Dare I hope your evening went better?" he says.

I head up the stairs to join him. "Pour me a drink, and I'll tell you all about it."

"It smells as if you've already had a few."

"Is that judgment of my drinking habits, Gray?"

"No, it's knowledge of your drinking habits, which suggests you may regret another."

"It was a few sips of a pint to be polite," I say.

"The glass was dirty?"

I sigh. "It always is."

"Poor Mallory. Let me get you a proper drink, then, clean glass and all."

FROM WHAT MY visit to the print shop suggested, we're not looking for someone who seriously intends to sell the letters. If they had thought they could, they don't seem to have made any inquiries to that effect. So we're most likely dealing with someone who fully expects Lady Inglis to pay. This is useful because it suggests some knowledge of her finances. As she said, five hundred pounds certainly isn't pocket change. It seems to be about as much as someone could expect to pay. Otherwise, they'd be left with letters they can't actually sell.

Of course, that could all be pure luck—they just happened to pick the right figure—which is why our first stop the next day is to the suspect least likely to know Lady Inglis's finances.

It seems early to be calling on an actress. They're not known for being morning people, especially in this era, when an ingenue like Miss Howell might be picking up some cash on the side. Not the sex trade per se, but entertaining—providing a pretty bit of scenery for a late-night party.

However, what kept Gray out late last night wasn't only inconsiderate clients. It was the stop he made afterward, to what seems to have been a far less staid sort of gentlemen's club than the one I got a peek at earlier.

It can be hard to remember that Gray is only my age. He seems older, with the weight of his era and his responsibilities. But he is

SCHEMES & SCANDALS

a young man and a bachelor at that, and so I don't doubt he knows where to go for late-night entertainment, the sort with gaming tables and actresses on their off nights.

From there, he learned that Miss Howell was not known to frequent such establishments...or any other sorts of establishments that might be popular with pretty young women whose acting careers don't pay the bills. Miss Howell actually has a day job working in a dress shop.

That is where I find her, and not even in the front, where I'd expect to find a pretty and poised young actress. She's in the back, working with several seamstresses. Even when the shop girl calls her forward, I think there's been a mistake. The young woman presented to me is small and plain looking, with the sort of red hair that isn't quite as flattering as Isla's.

When the clerk summons her, I say, "Miss Mary Howell?"

"Yes?"

"I am terribly sorry to bother you. It is about Lord Simpson. Might I speak with you outside? I am very sorry for the interruption."

She gives no sign of confusion or consternation and only smiles. "I will not refuse the excuse for a break. Yes, let us walk."

We head outside. Gray has stayed on the street for this interview. It makes more sense for me to speak to Miss Howell alone. I still spot him dressed in a shabby jacket and cap to blend in as well as he can. He'll tail us, but he's been warned to keep his distance. It's midday, and I doubt I need protection from Miss Howell.

"I wish to say in advance that Lord Simpson did not send me," I say. "I was given your name by another, and Lord Simpson will be piqued to hear we have spoken."

KELLEY ARMSTRONG

She frowns at me. "I have trouble even imagining Charlie in a state of pique, and if this would upset him, I am not certain we should speak."

"He has had an item go missing," I say. "My employer and I have been hired to find it."

She brightens at that. "Are you Pinkertons?"

There'd been a time when I'd have been flattered by the question. To young Mallory, the Pinkertons were swashbuckling American Wild West detectives. Sherlock Holmes on horseback, with a pair of six guns at his side. I know better after having chosen the Pinkertons for a high-school history report. While I'm sure there were real detectives among them, they were union breakers and corporate thugs, hired to protect the wealthy, not the innocent.

I laugh softly. "Not quite. We are private investigators of a much more discreet nature."

Her eyes still glimmer. "Detectives? Oh, please tell me you are a detective. I am an actress, and my company is putting on a murder play, with a woman detective, and I wanted the part, but the director says the only women detectives are elderly spinsters."

"You can tell him he is wrong. Anyone may be a detective, and the best are the ones no one expects, which may be elderly spinsters or..." I gesture at myself.

"Oh, this is terribly exciting. You say Charlie has lost something?" Her eyes round. "No, you said it had been stolen. And he did not wish to give my name because that would imply I could have stolen it. That is very sweet of him, but most shortsighted. In a proper mystery, one cannot rule out suspects simply because one does not wish to accuse them."

SCHEMES & SCANDALS

"Quite so. It is a delicate situation, and I understand why he did not wish to give your name, but I hope you recognize why we needed to find and speak to you."

"Of course."

"It is even more delicate because the item stolen belonged to another woman of Lord Simpson's acquaintance."

"Lady Inglis?" At my expression, she laughs. "That is the only other woman of his acquaintance at the moment, at least in the manner in which I presume you mean. I can certainly see why you would need to speak to me, though. If a man's...womanly friend loses an object at his home, his other womanly friend would be the primary suspect."

"Whoever this other woman is, she did not give your name, either."

A soft, trilling laugh. "You do not need to be quite so discreet, lass, but I understand why you feel the need. I am glad to hear that this other lady did not name me as a suspect. She is truly lovely, is she not?"

The genuine warmth in her voice gives me pause.

"Oh, apologies," she says with a sidelong grin. "Should I hiss and show my claws at the mention of the other woman in Charlie's life? I am sorry to disappoint you, but the situation is far less dramatic. This other lady being in Charlie's life is a blessing. It means I can rest confident that I am getting exactly what I want, a companion for when I wish companionship. Nothing more."

When I don't respond immediately, she says, "That is not what you expect, either, is it? After all, I am an actress, only

137

KELLEY ARMSTRONG

on the stage in hopes of securing a wealthy man to whisk me off it."

She grins. "If that were the case, I have chosen very poorly. No, I realize that is what people expect of actresses, but sadly, it is also what men expect. They fall in love with us on the stage, but to them, it is like seeing a pretty doll in a window. They do not wish us to stay on the stage. That is only the display case. Once they choose us, we are to give it up and live tucked away in comfort." She glances at me. "Comfort and abject boredom."

I smile. "It does sound rather dull."

"It would be. I will admit, I do not always intend to be a seamstress, but only because I aspire to make a proper career as an actress, which will not happen if I am a kept woman."

"Or a wife."

Another trilled laugh. "Heavens, no. Fortunately, I do not need to worry about either of those things with Charlie. If he wanted a wife, he'd marry the woman whose name we are not saying." She purses her lips. "If she'd have him, which she will not. But he would not marry me, and he cannot afford to keep me, so I am free to enjoy what he does offer."

I consider which avenue to pursue first. "You said his other lady friend will not have him?"

"Sadly, no. Sadly for poor Charlie, that is. Not sadly for the lady in question, as I do not blame her for not wanting another husband. If I were a widow with money, I would never marry again. I would simply take lovers."

"You are under the impression that Lord Simpson would like to marry her?"

SCHEMES & SCANDALS

Here, Miss Howell loses a little of her sparkle, retreating into a solemn, "That is not for me to say, miss, and as I cannot see how it relates to any missing item, I should not speculate."

"Understood and, as you say, inconsequential. You also said he cannot afford to keep you." I smile at her. "I presume you would be expensive."

Her good nature returns at that. "*Dreadfully* expensive. I would require oranges and strawberries year round."

"Which is more than Lord Simpson could afford?"

She sighs. "The poor fellow. I am only glad that he is still able to go abroad, as he planned. I had begun to worry he would need to cancel the trip. But the situation seems not as dire as he feared."

"Are you going abroad with him?"

"Heavens, no. That he could *certainly* not afford. Nor could I afford the time away from either of my jobs. No, I will travel one day, lass, but it will be to step on the stages of the world."

"Sounds lovely," I say. "Where would you most like to visit?"

She answers, and we finish our walk in amicable discussion of the places we'd love to travel.

"I DO NOT like the sound of that," Gray says morosely as I tell him about the interview.

"Yep."

"We had contradictory accounts of Lord Simpson's finances from his brother and the valet. I was inclined to believe his brother was mistaken."

KELLEY ARMSTRONG

"That Lord Simpson was just crying poor to keep his money from Arthur? That's what I hoped."

"You will want me to investigate his financial situation, then?"

"Yes, and I'll let you set that ball in motion before we pursue a bit of science."

He glances at me.

"It's time to check that ransom note for fingerprints," I say.

Fifteen

IT'S TEATIME when Jack—dressed in her maid clothes—comes into the laboratory to tell us our guest has arrived. Our other guest, that is. Our first guest joined us earlier this afternoon for the fingerprint analysis, as he has requested—possibly demanded—to be present anytime we need to do such a thing.

We leave him behind and meet Lord Simpson just inside the front door.

"What's this about, Gray?" Simpson says, and Miss Howell might not have been able to imagine him piqued, but he definitely seems piqued right now.

I step forward. "Thank you so much for joining us. We do appreciate you coming on such short notice, sir." I pause and then say, "I fear it is about your valet, and we wished you to hear this in person."

"My *former* valet?" Simpson exhales. "He stole the letters, didn't he? You could have just said that, instead of summoning me to speak on a 'delicate matter' in regards to your investigation."

"It *is* delicate," I say. "Now, if you will permit our maid to take your coat, we shall have tea upstairs and explain the situation fully."

GRAY, SIMPSON, AND I have settled in the drawing room, where Jack has served tea. I wait until we've started to eat, then I exclaim, "Oh! Lord Simpson, that plate is not supposed to be used. It has a crack." I rise and put out my hand. "Can you pass it to me, please?"

He does, with some confusion, and I give him a fresh plate from a stack on the sideboard. Then I sit back down.

Gray clears his throat. "About your valet…"

"Yes," Simpson says. "You believe he is responsible for this, but I assure you, I cannot see it."

"Because you offered to pay the blackmail if he was."

Simpson pauses. "Yes."

"That is what we wished to speak to you about. The fact that you offered to pay—and did not tell us—meant we went into the interview missing vital information. We need everything, Charles."

Simpson sighs. "So you have summoned me to rap my knuckles? Fine. I deserved that. I could not help myself. Lewis was the obvious suspect, and so I had to be sure."

"And how did you intend to pay him, should he have been the culprit?"

Simpson stops with his teacup raised. "Hmm?"

SCHEMES & SCANDALS

"This is the other delicate part of this meeting," Gray says. "We had several accounts that your finances are in disorder, and so I investigated, because it seemed odd that you would attempt to pay your valet five hundred pounds if you did not have such funds at hand."

"You investigated my—"

"Yes." Gray meets his gaze. "We are investigators. That is what we do. It appears you have recently defaulted on a loan. It also appears that you have planned a trip to Europe but have not paid for it."

"How the devil—?"

A knock at the door. Gray calls a greeting. It opens, and McCreadie walks in, having only come from downstairs, though he rubs his hands, as if still warming them from the winter cold.

"Hugh," Gray says. "How good of you to join us. Hugh, this is Lord Simpson. Lord Simpson, this is my good friend, Detective McCreadie, criminal officer of the Edinburgh Police."

Simpson visibly blanches before daubing his lips with his napkin and rising to shake McCreadie's hand.

"It seems you have another guest, Duncan," Simpson says. "I shall take my leave—"

"No, Detective McCreadie is here on business. And has shown up just in time for tea." Gray waves to the fourth spot, which Simpson obviously hadn't noticed was set.

"Have you heard of finger marks?" Gray says. "And their applications to criminal science?"

Simpson looks at McCreadie, as if this question is clearly intended for him.

143

KELLEY ARMSTRONG

"I am asking you, Charles," Gray says.

"Me? I know nothing of criminal science."

"But you said the other day that you wished to know more about my cases and the application of science in them, and so I thought you might find this interesting. If you look at your finger-tips, you'll see tiny ridges in fascinating patterns. No two people's patterns are alike."

Simpson's brows rise as he looks at his fingertips. "They are unique?"

"Yes. In fact, for well over a century, China has used finger marks as an acceptable substitute for contractual signatures. Japan has used them. India has also used them. We are slower here, but European scientists have been studying finger marks for over a century."

"That is fascinating," Simpson says, in a tone that suggests he's simply being polite.

"Finger marks are everywhere," I say. "Every time we touch something, we leave our mark, quite literally. Like this plate." I gesture at the one I took from him. "You touched one side, so your prints are there. I touched the other. Mine are there."

"And the maid's are all over it," Simpson says, with an easy smile. "The maid's, the cook's… I can only imagine how many of these finger marks are on it."

"Only the two sets," I say. "It was cleaned before we ate." I look at Simpson. "Would you like a demonstration? I can show you the marks."

"That's hardly necessary. While this is all very interesting, we are in the midst of tea—"

"Detective McCreadie? Would you assist me?"

SCHEMES & SCANDALS

I produce four blank cards and a stamp pad that Gray helped me devise. With McCreadie's help, I roll my fingertips in the ink and press them onto the cards. Then I do the same to take Gray and McCreadie's prints. Simpson hesitates, but then he decides to be a good sport and lets me take his prints, which saves me from needing to use the ones on the plate.

"So these are your fingerprints," I say, holding up the card. "Earlier, we conducted the same experiment on the ransom note Lady Inglis received."

Now Simpson stops short. "What?"

"Detective McCreadie? May I have that card?"

He produces an envelope, and I open it with all due drama. "We lifted two sets of prints. One belonged to Lady Inglis, who provided an exemplar so we could exclude hers. The other..." I lay it down beside the card with Simpson's print. "Hmm... Am I correct, Detective McCreadie? Do these match?"

I knew they would. I'd memorized a part of the pattern from the letter and noted the match as soon as I took Simpson's prints. If it hadn't been a match, I'd have just pretended this was a very peculiar piece of teatime entertainment.

"It is indeed a match," McCreadie says, his gaze rising to Simpson.

Simpson blusters. "Because I touched it. When Patricia showed me. I held the note."

"No, you didn't," I say. "We asked about that before we took it. Only Lady Inglis handled it. She read it to you aloud and then returned it to the envelope, which she immediately put into her safe, along with the letter."

KELLEY ARMSTRONG

There are several ways Simpson could play this. The most obvious is to call bullshit on the science. Most people would—it's not even admissible in court yet. But there's a reason Gray liked Simpson. The viscount is a curious and intelligent man, interested in science. He is a believer, and so it never occurs to him to call this bullshit. He knows it isn't.

Instead, his gaze goes straight to McCreadie. "I stole nothing. The letter from Lady Inglis was my own property, and therefore, I cannot be charged with theft."

"Hugh was only here to witness the fingermark identification," Gray says. "Unless you wish to press the point—and have him agree it was not theft, but it *was* blackmail, which is also illegal."

"The situation is not as it seems," Simpson says.

Gray only nods, but some offenders need only the vaguest hint of empathy to unburden themselves. As a detective, I interviewed suspects where I couldn't bring myself to fake empathy, but sometimes, even a nod was enough.

"I am not a bad person," Simpson says. "You know that, Duncan. I care very much for Patricia. The problem is... Blast it, this was never supposed to go so far."

I open my mouth, but he's not looking at me. Not looking at McCreadie. His confession is for Gray alone.

"You expected her to pay," Gray says.

"Yes, blast it. She has the money. I was very careful about that. I would not have asked for more than she could afford. I never thought she'd bring someone else into it. It wasn't as if she would take such a case to the police."

SCHEMES & SCANDALS

Because she'd be too ashamed. It wasn't only the amount he'd been careful about. He'd chosen a method of blackmail designed to shame Lady Inglis—his lover, his friend—into paying.

It's probably a good thing Simpson only has eyes for Gray right now, because if he looked my way, I'm not sure I could hide my disgust and outrage well enough to keep him confessing.

"You offered to pay the ransom because you knew she would never allow that," Gray says, still calm, his expression blank. "You also offered to pay your valet because you knew he didn't have the letters. And, if Lady Inglis accused him, as the obvious culprit, you could say you'd attempted to buy them back. That would stall any further investigation until it was too late."

Simpson had let the valet go at exactly the right time for Lewis to be the obvious culprit. Offering to buy back the letters would deliberately muddy the waters. Lady Inglis would think Lewis stole the letters, yet Simpson's offer seemed to prove otherwise, and the date for payment would arrive too quickly for her to make a decision. She'd be forced to pay.

"I would have repaid her," Simpson says.

"Then why not simply ask for a loan?" Gray says.

Frustration darkens Simpson's face. "Because I do not wish to be treated as a child. If I told Patricia that I needed money for my trip, she would say I do not need the trip. She does not understand that I *do* need it. My mind must be stimulated by travel, or I grow bored." His lips jut in something dangerously close to a pout. "I am poor company if I am bored."

I try not to stare at Simpson. Is this what it's like to be born into the nobility? To never need to work for a living? To not even

KELLEY ARMSTRONG

understand the difference between a want and a need? It all blurs together into your unalienable rights.

"I would have repaid it," he says, that lip jutting a little more. "So it *would* have been a loan."

"For which you threatened her with public humiliation," Gray says, his tone still deceptively mild.

"I'd never do such a thing. Not to Patricia. Not to any woman. I am not that sort of man."

Gray says nothing. I inwardly seethe with all the things I want to say, all the things I can't say. Gray's silence speaks enough, and under it, Simpson squirms.

"I would never have exposed her," Simpson mutters. "The letters are all safe. No one has seen them."

"Good," Gray murmurs. "Then you shall return them to Lady Inglis."

Simpson perks up. "Yes, of course. I will quietly return them, and she need never know that I was the one—"

"No."

"I can still credit your investigation. Whoever stole them realized you were on the case and returned them to me in the post—"

"No."

"But you cannot tell her the truth," Simpson protests. "She will be hurt, and there is no need—"

"Yes, there is." Gray meets his gaze. "The only question is *who* tells her the truth. You or me?"

Sixteen

E'RE AT Lady Inglis's house. Simpson never answered Gray's question. He'd gotten up and walked out.

Gray had given him twelve hours. He did ask me about that, and I can grumble that his "consultation" came after he'd made up his mind, but I'll give him this on the grounds that the parties involved are his casual friend and his former lover. They are also members of the nobility. Gray must take care where he places each step to avoid landmines.

Gray and Isla might choose to step on some of those social landmines, but it's a calculated decision with equally calculated efforts to avoid stomping on enough of them to make life in this world untenable.

The next morning, we go to see Lady Inglis. If I'm to cut Gray a break in not consulting me on the timeline, I suspect that if it weren't for me, he'd have given Simpson a full day, possibly even waited until after tomorrow, which is Hogmanay. Yes, that's the deadline for the ransom, but I've already notified Lady Inglis that

KELLEY ARMSTRONG

she doesn't need to pay. Waiting until after the holiday would be the more socially correct thing to do, but in moving sooner, Gray is acknowledging that this is my investigation. And, maybe, he's also acknowledging that while letting Lady Inglis enjoy Hogmanay in blissful ignorance may seem a mercy, I don't think she's the kind of person who would appreciate that. I know I wouldn't.

I suggest Gray go alone. It may be my investigation, but this is still a personal-adjacent matter that might be easier without me there. He asks me to attend, though, and I can tell that's not just Gray being polite. He's uncomfortable visiting Lady Inglis on his own.

I do suggest he tell her in private. We don't know whether Simpson has confessed. I suspect not. Either way, it will be easier for Lady Inglis to hear it from Gray alone.

I sit in the parlor while they go into another room. This time, I make sure the doors are shut and I can't hear any of their conversation. When the clock strikes the half hour, Gray emerges. He shoots me the smallest shake of his head, which means no, Simpson did not confess. Coward.

Lady Inglis appears a moment later, smiling with false brightness, her eyes red rimmed from tears.

"Miss Mitchell," she says. "If I might speak to you, we may conclude our business."

"That isn't necessary, ma'am. We can finish this up in the new year. I will leave you to your day."

"I insist." She tries for that smile again. "I would like to thank you. Duncan? Would you please have someone fetch your coat?"

Gray hesitates. He realizes he's being dismissed, and his gaze shoots to me. I nod, and he leaves with obvious reluctance.

SCHEMES & SCANDALS

"Miss Mitchell?" Lady Inglis says, and leads me into the adjoining room, which is...

Look, I can't tell one Victorian sitting area from another. Sitting room. Parlor. Drawing room. Unless it has books and I can clearly identify it as a library, I know it probably has a specific purpose—Victorian rooms always do—but to me, it's just another place where people sit and talk.

Oh, wait. Scratch that. This one has a piano. That makes it a music room. Of course, it also has chairs, which means it's probably mostly used for sitting and talking. Although, having been in a few of these while someone is playing the piano, I've discovered that just because there's live music doesn't mean people *don't* also sit and talk. It's like going to a piano bar...except the player is probably your poor spinster sister-in-law, whose job is to provide pleasant background music.

Lady Inglis walks to the piano, and for a second, I think she's going to sit down and play, but she only runs her fingers along the top of it. Then she looks up abruptly, as if having forgotten I'm there.

"I do appreciate you resolving this matter, Miss Mitchell," she says. "I realize it is an awkward conclusion, and there may have been some temptation to resolve it quietly, with me never knowing the truth, but I appreciate the honesty. I would not have wanted to be coddled with lies."

"Dr. Gray thought you deserved to know." I don't add that I agree—there's no need to insert myself here.

She smiles a little wistfully. "Of course he did. He is a good man."

"He is."

She looks toward the window. "I suppose you think me foolish."

KELLEY ARMSTRONG

"Not at all. Lord Simpson is very charming, and everyone we spoke to had nothing but praise for him."

"Oh, I do not mean that." Her smile turns my way, rueful now. "I am disappointed in Charles but, perhaps, not as shocked as I should be. I recognize his flaws, and I always thought they did not affect me unless I married him, which I had no intention of doing. I misjudged. That is my fault."

She sighs as she walks to the window. "I have known for a while that the affair ought to end. I may retain him as a friend, if that is possible, but otherwise..." She shrugs. "While I loved my husband very much, I was young when we married, and after his death, I wanted to experience a different sort of life. That whim is passing, and I fear in a few years, I shall be much too dull for Charlie's tastes, an aging widow with more interest in her charities and foundations than the latest gossip and balls."

She gazes out the window long enough that I eye the door, wondering whether I'm supposed to leave.

"When I said you must think me foolish, I was referring to Duncan," she says finally, still looking out. "You are aware I had a past with him?"

She glances over and then nods before I can say anything, as if my expression answered for me. "I thought as much. That is where I was foolish."

She turns fully my way. "Shortly after I met Duncan, I made the mistake of saying I knew French. What I meant is that I know enough French to give instructions to a maid in a Paris hotel. He bought me a book in French—about Renaissance art, which is an area of interest for me. I could barely decipher five words per page.

SCHEMES & SCANDALS

That book reminds me of Duncan himself. He is a story written in another language, one I do not know. One I pretended to know."

She walks across the room. "I never knew where I stood with Duncan, what he truly thought of me, and so I made mistakes. Silly mistakes more becoming an infatuated girl than a grown woman. I am not certain why I did what I did. To make him jealous and force some admission of caring? Or to pretend I did not feel any depth of emotion for him myself?"

She makes a face and waves her hand. "You have no idea what I mean, and I'm prattling. My point is that I *was* foolish. I hurt him, and I lost him, and I know I am not getting him back." She meets my gaze. "Do not make the same mistake, Miss Mitchell."

"Dr. Gray and I are not—"

"Not currently involved. I know, and if I ever thought otherwise, that was my jealousy speaking. Duncan would not employ a young woman with any other intentions. But you are more than that pretty face, and he is clearly fond of you. Consider me a soothsayer peering into the future and offering you a warning. Do not mistake his seeming lack of emotion for an actual lack of it. He does feel, and he can be hurt."

Yes, I know that. I could say so, but there's no point. This is advice offered genuinely, and it applies even to friendship, so I can take it as that, with only a solemn nod and a "Thank you, ma'am."

"Good." She brightens, but it's still forced, the look in her eyes a little lost before she finds purpose with, "Let us get you paid. Best to settle my accounts before the year's end."

Seventeen

IT'S THE last day of the year, and Gray and I are enjoying a day of rest. Okay, "enjoying" might be an exaggeration. Possibly even sarcasm. It isn't even noon yet, and we're already at loose ends.

Any festivities won't begin until this evening, which means we have the whole day to do whatever we want. Except... Well, we can't do what we want because before Isla left on last-minute errands with Mrs. Wallace, she made us promise not to do any work. At all. We can't crack open a jar from Gray's collection of pickled body parts. We aren't even supposed to set foot in the laboratory. Gray can't work on his latest paper for publication. I can't catch up on reading his past publications. If it is even tangentially related to the triumvirate of work—undertaking, forensic science, or detection—we are forbidden to engage in it, which seems more like a punishment than a gift.

As for gifts, I'm still short one for Isla, which means I need to go shopping, but Isla also made me promise to keep an eye on her brother and make sure he doesn't work. I have a feeling that's

KELLEY ARMSTRONG

supposed to go both ways. If I need to watch him, then I also can't sneak in any work. But if he's supposed to be relaxing, then last-minute holiday shopping with me isn't what she had in mind.

While we've been reading, there's really a limit to how long either of us can do that without getting antsy. So when the door-bell rings, we practically bowl each other over in our haste to answer. Jack is running last-minute errands while Alice is with Isla and Mrs. Wallace, meaning we are left to answer the door...or fight over who gets the privilege. I manage to throw it open first, with Gray right at my heels.

It's a young man with a thick envelope. "Package for Miss Mallory Mitchell."

"That is me. Thank you." I take it and turn to Gray. "Pay the lad, sir."

"For *your* package?"

He doesn't hesitate, though, and gives the young man enough to set the boy grinning. After the door is shut, Gray whisks the envelope from my hand.

"Fine," I say. "I will repay you."

"That is not my concern. My concern is that this almost certainly contains work, and we are not to work today."

I reach for the envelope. "Let me open it and find out."

He holds it aloft. "I cannot allow you to take that chance. In merely opening it, you might lay eyes on correspondence of a work nature and thus break your vow to Isla. I will save you from that. You may have this the day after tomorrow."

I glare and grab for it, but he easily holds it above my head.

"Pity you are not taller," he says. "If only you could reach— Ow!"

SCHEMES & SCANDALS

He dances back, lifting his knee. "Did you just kick your employer in the shin?"

"Certainly not." I pluck the envelope from his hand. "I am forbidden to work today, so you cannot be my employer."

"That isn't how it works."

I peer up at him. "Is it not? So you are always my employer? Always in a position of authority, ready to wield it over me even on a rare full day off? How very Victorian of you."

"That..." He fixes me with a look. "That is unfair."

"Nope." I walk off, holding the envelope. "See, now if you'd accused me of kicking a *friend* in the shins, I'd have felt bad. But an employer who insists on being treated as an employer even when I am not working? *He* deserves a kick in the shins."

"Who is the package from?" he says as I head for the stairs.

"Such an employer also does not deserve to share in the temporary distraction of *my* unexpected mail."

I'm halfway up the stairs when Gray snatches the envelope from my hands. I wheel and nearly stumble straight into his arms. He manages to catch me.

"Trying to trip me on the stairs now?" I say.

"I just saved your life. You could have fallen and broken your neck."

"Only because you—" I shake my head. "The envelope, please."

"Am I allowed to witness the opening?"

"If you can be quiet and patient. Which means no."

He shakes his head and hands it over. We continue up and back into the library, where I sit. Then I open the envelope to find a sheaf of papers. I flip through the sheets and frown.

KELLEY ARMSTRONG

"It seems to be a manuscript," I say. "How odd. Who would…?" I trail off as I see the letter on top.

Dear Miss Mitchell,

I very much enjoyed meeting you and Dr. Gray, and I would love to learn more about your joint efforts in the science of detection. Might I take you both to dinner next year, when I visit Edinburgh in the summer?

In the meantime, here are the first chapters of my new book. I have even signed it. I thought it might be an appropriate Hogmanay gift for Dr. Gray's sister.

All the brightest blessings in the new year. May 1870 be wonderful for you both.

Faithfully yours,

Charles Dickens

I stare at the letter as my eyes fill. Then I hand the papers to Gray and go to look out the window over the rear gardens.

"Mallory?" Gray says, his voice soft. "Are you all right?"

"I am overcome by his kindness, that is all."

His hand closes on my elbow, making me jump, but I don't turn.

"That is not all," he murmurs.

I shake my head.

"Mr. Dickens will not be taking us to dinner next year, will he?" Gray's voice is so soft that it breaks the dam, tears flowing even as I wipe them away.

"I wondered if that was it," Gray says. "You were very kind when we spoke to him, but I could tell something was wrong.

SCHEMES & SCANDALS

When he spoke about his new book, you...seemed distressed. I did not know whether to speak of it again later. I realize there are things you know that...we should not."

I nod, still looking out the window.

"Might we talk of it?" he murmurs. "Since I have figured it out for myself?"

I hesitate, and then I turn. "I didn't know until he mentioned what he was writing, and then I realized what it was and that he'll never finish it and..."

Gray pulls me into a hug. It's a careful movement, gently tugging me and checking for any resistance. I let myself fall onto his shoulder, and he pats my back, a little awkwardly.

"I'm overreacting," I say.

"Not at all."

"I don't know Mr. Dickens beyond his work. I shouldn't be so rattled by knowing he's going to die soon. I just..." I take a deep breath and blurt, "It reminds me of watching the hanging."

I expect him to ask how, but he only nods and says, "You see a living person and know they're going to die."

"Which happened with my nan, too. I knew she was dying. I was there when she did. But it felt different. I helped put someone on the gallows and watched her die. Saw her speak, knowing she would be dead in a few minutes. She was a horrible person, but still..."

"Yes."

After I'd gone to the execution, Gray told me that he'd accompanied McCreadie to a couple, when McCreadie had to stand as witness. Like me, he thought he'd been prepared, and then discovered he wasn't.

KELLEY ARMSTRONG

"And Mr. Dickens *isn't* a horrible person," I say. "He didn't kill anyone. But somehow, because I know he's dying soon, I feel as if I'm responsible. It wasn't like that with my nan."

"Because in Mr. Dickens's case, you possess knowledge no one else does."

"I can't stop his death," I say. "In case you're wondering."

"I would never wonder that," he says softly.

"It's a stroke. Maybe he already feels poorly and that's why he's retiring from the performances." I glance at the letter. "So, yes, that has been weighing on my mind, and I apologize if I've been testy."

His lips quirk. "If you were, I presumed I gave you cause, as usual."

He sobers and steps back. "In this case, I *did* give you cause, and I would like to apologize for that. I insisted on hearing Lady Inglis out regarding the case, and then I snapped at your every attempt to make the situation easier for me."

"Yes," I say, but then add, "I understand it was difficult for you."

"Which is why you tried to mitigate that." He walks across the library and lowers himself to a chair with a sigh. "I thought I could emotionally detach myself from it, but I could not."

I know what I should say, and I don't want to. But if I really am his friend, then I need to.

I settle into the seat next to his and turn to him. "If you regret how things ended…"

"I do."

I tamp down the blaze of disappointment.

"You could reverse that," I say.

SCHEMES & SCANDALS

He frowns over at me, brows creasing. "Reverse…?"

"If you still have feelings for Lady Inglis, I strongly suspect they would be reciprocated."

He lets out a deep sigh and slumps into his chair. "Which is both the problem and *not* the problem. The opposite of the problem, in fact."

"Okay…"

He slants a look my way. "I am going to make a confession that will not reflect well on me. I was not entirely honest about how things ended. Yes, I made the mistake of thinking it was an exclusive relationship. Yes, I found out otherwise. Yes, that would have ended the relationship for me. However…"

He fusses in his seat before saying, "I may have given the impression I was angry, even hurt. I certainly behaved that way to Lady Inglis. But that is a lie. I was relieved."

"Relieved?"

His hands move on his lap, as if he's not sure what to do with them. "When it happened, I discovered I was relieved to have a reason to end the affair. I enjoyed her company, but we did not suit, and instead of politely disengaging, I leapt on an excuse."

He glances my way. "An excuse that could be seen as her fault. Which was not my intention at the time. I took full responsibility for the misunderstanding. I thought that would be the end of things. However, the problem with blaming a misunderstanding is that it leaves the other party thinking that the problem can be rectified."

"Ah," I say. "Lady Inglis wanted to fix things. That's why she sent the letter and such."

KELLEY ARMSTRONG

A slight flush touches his cheeks. "Yes, and the more she tried to reunite, the worse I felt." He takes a deep breath. "I treated her poorly."

"Not as poorly as Lord Simpson did."

A humorless smile. "That is not much consolation, given how horrified I am by his actions. It also compounds the matter. She deserves better."

"She does," I say. "And I hope she finds it. What you did…"

I consider before I continue. "I understand that you feel bad for misleading her, but I also understand why you did. Is it ever possible to break up with someone and *not* hurt their feelings? There's a breakup cliché in my world. The person ending things often says 'It's not you, it's me' in hopes of making it easier. Because how do you tell someone you just don't fancy them enough?"

"Yes. I was fond of her. I enjoyed our time together, and she was a good person who did nothing wrong." He exhales. "So that is my confession. If I was uncomfortable during this case, it was because I had done wrong by her. I could fix that by confessing… but it feels as if it would only make things worse."

"Yeah, going back and saying you just weren't that into her definitely *isn't* going to make her feel better. We solved her case, and from what I understand, that pushed her to make a choice she already knew she had to make." I glance at him. "Like discovering she was still seeing Lord Simpson pushed you to make a choice you knew you had to make. Sometimes we need the push. Now I hope she finds someone who treats her as she deserves to be treated."

"As do I."

SCHEMES & SCANDALS

I rise and take the envelope from the table. "Circling back to this, Mr. Dickens wanted me to give the first chapters to Isla, but I don't feel right doing that."

"Because he'll never finish the book."

I nod. "I think, after his death, I can give this to her and explain."

"She would like that very much."

I pass him a wry smile. "I still need to get her a gift, though."

His brows shoot up. "You have not—" He winces. "Of course you haven't. You have been busy on the case I dragged you into."

"You didn't drag, and thanks to that case, I can get her something nice. I just..." I glance at the window, the light already fading. "I need to do it fast."

"Let us go out together, then."

Eighteen

THAT EVENING is a true delight. I might not have gotten the Victorian Christmas I envisioned, but this is even better. It resurrects wonderful memories of my nan and our Hogmanay celebrations together, while building new memories for this new life.

We start with a feast that's half Scottish and half Dickens's *Christmas Carol*, with haggis and roast goose and mincemeat and black buns. Even Jack decides to stay for this part, though she'll leave later to meet up with friends. McCreadie comes to dinner, as does Annis.

Once the meal is eaten, we all help with the cleanup, over Mrs. Wallace's protests—I get the sense this is an annual mini-drama, with everyone knowing their lines. Once the dishes are done and the kitchen is clean, Isla presents all the staff with the traditional Hogmanay gift of new clothes, which we wear that night to symbolize a new year and new beginnings. As I put on my dress, I discovered a pound note in each pocket, which is apparently another tradition to ward off misfortune, presumably of the financial sort.

KELLEY ARMSTRONG

From there, we go into the streets where the party is heating up…quite literally. There are endless torches and bonfires, and the others indulge my love of fireballs by joining a parade. The evening proceeds up to Calton Hill, where we watch boats below, which have been, yep, set on fire.

We end the celebrations at midnight with Molotov cocktails—yes, that's my fault, too. Then Simon, Alice, and Mrs. Wallace stay behind at the town house, and Annis returns home, while Gray, Isla, McCreadie, and I go to McCreadie's apartment so Gray can be first over the threshold.

According to Scottish custom, the first foot over the door sets the luck for the year, and the most lucky guest of all is a tall and dark-haired man. My nan said this hearkened back to Viking days, when finding a blond dude on your doorstep was really bad luck. Gray does the first-footing every year for McCreadie, taking his friend a gift of salt and a black bun. Then we all go inside to exchange gifts.

It's nearly three when we get home, a little tipsy and a little giddy. Gray stays to share a drink with Simon, which also lets him serve as the first-footer for Simon's apartment.

"I have another gift for you," I say to Isla once we're inside.

"More? You were overly generous already."

I wave that off. "This is just a little extra. It's in my room."

We make our way up, and I pass her a package wrapped in brown paper. "Jack and I visited a print shop during the investigation, and I bought you some samples."

She slowly takes the package. "Given what you were there to investigate, do I want to know what sort of 'samples' you bought me?"

SCHEMES & SCANDALS

"Warming material."

She arches an eyebrow. "Warming material?"

"Scottish winters are very long, very dark, and very cold. That might make them a little more tolerable."

Her cheeks go bright red, and she feigns a scowl.

"You just like to see me blush, don't you?" she says.

"You blush very prettily."

Her eyes narrow. "And you are a very poor liar."

"Happy Hogmanay, Isla."

She looks at me. Then she puts her arms out, and I fall into her hug.

"Happy Hogmanay, Mallory."

I AM IN the kitchen by dawn, having entreated Alice to get me up, no matter how tired or hungover I am. I still have one gift left to give, and while I convinced Mrs. Wallace to lend me her kitchen for it, I can't rely on her to wake me.

Mrs. Wallace may have granted me the kitchen—or a piece of countertop and a burner on the stove—but that doesn't keep her from grumbling about my "nonsense." I ignore her and spend the next two hours working, past the time when Alice rushes in to say, "They are awake, ma'am!" and Mrs. Wallace kicks into high gear preparing the first breakfast of the new year.

Once I'm ready, I race upstairs to change as quickly as I can. Luckily, I already put on all my undergarments and only need to

KELLEY ARMSTRONG

switch out my dress, wash my face and adjust my hair. Then it's back down to the kitchen to get the gift.

I walk into the dining room just as Gray is saying to Isla, "Is Mallory not joining us?"

"Mallory is right here," I say. "Mallory had to get up at an ungodly hour to make your gift."

I set the platter in front of him. On it are a half dozen still-warm pastries.

"Doughnuts," I say. "I can't tell whether they're a thing yet, but if they are, they're an American thing."

Isla leans forward and inhales. "They smell delicious."

"They're for you, too," I say. "Duncan gets first pick. Those two are dusted with cinnamon sugar." I point. "Those two are jam filled, and the other two are my attempt at a chocolate glaze, which is tricky here."

I take my seat. "They're basically fried dough. I went through a phase of making them as a teen, and I remember the recipe. *And* I can get all the ingredients here and make them without an electric oven."

Isla sighs. "Do not tease me again with talk of electric ovens and electric ice boxes."

I could ask when's the last time she actually used the oven here, but I hold my tongue and turn to Gray. "If you don't like them, please feel free to say so. I have a couple more recipes I could try."

"And if I do like them?" he says.

"Then I'll make you a batch every month. One plateful wouldn't be a proper gift. Although, you might need to speak to

168

SCHEMES & SCANDALS

Mrs. Wallace if you want that—the biggest problem making these was getting her to give up part of her kitchen this morning."

He takes his fork and cuts off a piece, and I don't correct his process. One bite, and then another, and then another.

I try not to hold my breath awaiting the verdict. Of course I do. This isn't the fanciest gift I could get him, but I put more thought and effort into it than I care to admit.

"There is one problem," he says as he takes a bite of the next one.

My heart thuds. "Okay."

"I will tell Mrs. Wallace that you need to commandeer her kitchen once a month, but you are going to need to explain why I do not eat her carefully prepared breakfast this morning."

He glances at Isla. "You will need to wait and try next month's batch. *These* are all mine."

She rolls her eyes, reaches over and snatches one, and I relax and settle in to watch them eat as they chatter and laugh.

1869 has been a hell of a year, and I'm still reeling, as much as I try to pretend otherwise. But it's no longer 1869. Today is the first day of 1870, and I'm still here, no longer a guest but a citizen.

While I've never been one to make resolutions, this year, I will. It's time to make this my world. Find my place and settle in, because I'm not going anywhere.

I snake a hand out to grab a doughnut from Gray's plate. He tries to grab it back, but I take a quick bite before holding it out.

"Still want it?" I say.

He eyes the bitten doughnut. "I ought to say no but…"

KELLEY ARMSTRONG

I laugh, cut it in half and give him the piece without the bite. Then I settle in with my pastry and my coffee and listen to Isla and Gray making plans for the day. Plans for *our* day, together.

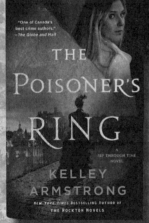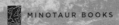